DEVLIN'S HOLLOW

I0551882

Terence West

DEVLIN'S HOLLOW

GRAVESTONE PRESS

A GRAVESTONE PRESS PAPERBACK

© Copyright 2007
Terence West

The right of Terence West to be identified as author of
this work has been asserted in accordance with the
Copyright, Designs and Patents Act 1988

All Rights Reserved

No reproduction, copy or transmission of the publication
may be made without written permission. No paragraph
of this publication may be reproduced, copied or
transmitted save with the written permission of the
publisher, or in accordance with the provisions of the
Copyright Act 1956 (as amended).

Any person who does any unauthorised act in relation to
this publication may be liable to criminal prosecution
and civil claims for damages.

ISBN 978-1-78695-691-0

Gravestone Press
is an imprint of
Fiction4All

This Edition Published 2021
Fiction4All
www.fiction4all.com

Inspired by a true story.

Dedication

For Rose:
You've helped me find a man I thought I lost and never stopped believing in me. Thank you.

Chapter One

Static assaulted my ears.

Tapping the volume key, a cacophony of white noise spilled into my headphones and encased me within the folds of its undulating, jagged interior. My eyes danced across the peaks and valleys of a green digital waveform on the display before me as each aural texture was given shape. Hitting the space bar with my thumb, I stopped playback, relishing a moment of silence. Once I raised my hand, I massaged my tired neck. A nasty stress headache was beginning to slither up my spine and settle in my skull.

Furrowing my brow, I moved the cursor back roughly ten seconds and continued the track. What started as a hobby had evolved. Some would call it an obsession, but I was secretly hopeful it hadn't gone that far. Focusing on cutting through the digital sizzle, I pressed the phones tighter to my ears listening for anything buried in the sonic palette that shouldn't be there. I wasn't listening to the hiss, but rather the space between.

Rubbing the bridge of my nose with my fingers, I exhaled slowly. This wasn't helping. Maybe I was becoming obsessed. Spending all of my spare time listening to blank recordings and chasing after stories, myths, and legends was beginning to wear on me. I was searching for...hell, I didn't even know anymore. Answers? Proof? Or was it something more? Of course I already knew the answer to my own question, I simply didn't want to acknowledge it. To do so would make it more tangible, more real somehow, and I wasn't ready to accept that. Would that prove I was obsessed, or crazy? I was a man charging into the darkness with a flashlight and a tape recorder, in the pursuit of what could be nothing more than an idea.

I had gone mad…

…I just missed her so much.

Leaning my head back, I watched the picturesque suburban landscape of Union scroll outside my window. A little more than an hour from New York, this sleepy suburb seemed more like a different world than somehow part of the Big Apple. Cozy little houses enclosed by picket fences paraded past in unison as if marching to celebrate mediocrity. Trees reached perpetually toward the solid gray sky from snow-covered lawns, while children created an entire population of snowpeople locked in frozen poses. A myriad of cars passed in the opposite direction most likely headed home for a hug and a kiss from their loved ones as they basked in the glow of Christmas tree lights. It was all so…

Ordinary.

But very familiar…

Like an extraterrestrial trying to comprehend this bizarre form of life, I observed with awe. Their existence seemed somehow foreign to me. It was something I'd heard spoken of in whispers, but had never experienced myself. My vocation forced me to distance myself from humanity in order to effectively learn their behavior and mannerisms. I surveiled and recorded in some vain effort to unlock

8

the mysteries of the human brain. I felt like a spy, the snake in the garden, desperately wanting to be part of the hive.

My eyes fell to the light gray carpeting of the taxi's interior as the audio file continued to play in my headphones. Recorded in my home office, I had nearly nine hours to review. Having spent most of the plane trip analyzing it, I was about halfway through. I heard the familiar creaks, pops, and groans of the house settling, the wind howling outside, and a tree branch scraping against the windowpane, but little else. No signs, no voices, no phenomenon that could not be explained. There was nothing. Absolutely nothing.

The taxi driver's waving hand caught my attention. Unsure if he was signaling me or gesturing to another driver, I paused the recording. Sliding the big, black headphones down to my neck, I looked inquisitively at the cabbie.

"Just heard over the radio," the heavyset man motioned to the CB installed in his dash, "that Elmore is closed because of an accident. Some jackass t-boned a bus."

"What does that mean to us?"

"We have to go 'round," the big man reported in his Brooklyn accent. "Shouldn't take too long, just wanted to make sure that was all right wit' you."

"Yeah, yeah." I waved dismissively. "No worries. Do what you have to do."

Silence fell over the cab again. I considered pulling my headphones back on and continuing, but I couldn't seem to summon the will. Sliding my fingertips across the keyboard, I saved my progress and quit the program. I placed the laptop in hibernate and snapped the lid shut. Checking my wristwatch, I hoped the new route wouldn't delay us too long. I had scheduled my appointment weeks ago, and was already cutting it close.

The cabbie looked at me in his rearview mirror. "Sinatra?"

I took a moment to process the question, perplexed. "Pardon?"

"Sinatra," the portly man repeated through his bushy, gray mustache. "I bet you're listening to Sinatra."

I tried to force a smile. "You would have lost that bet, my friend."

The cabbie snapped his fingers and shrugged. "I only like the big band stuff. The Rat Pack, Sinatra, Sammy, Martin." He shrugged. "That's amore, you know?"

"I know the Rat Pack," I confirmed.

I glanced down at the driver's fact sheet attached to the back of his seat. His name was Ralph Chandler, a native of New York—as if I couldn't already tell. The picture in the upper left featured Ralph sporting a huge, shit-eating grin that looked as if he had just told the photographer the dirtiest joke he knew. I imagined him living in a tiny, rundown apartment with his wife Alice, and slightly crazy neighbor named Norton who always seemed to get into trouble. I smirked…don't ask me why. I was a bit of a pop culture junkie.

"That's some great friggin' music," Ralph added. "Classics!" He paused. "So what were you listening to?" He sized me up in the rearview mirror. "None of that new age, I-want-to-share-my-feelings, weepy, fairy music...right?"

I laughed despite myself. "No." I tried to stop laughing for fear I would snort. "No weepy, fairy music. EVPs," I admitted as if that would mean something to the cabbie.

As I suspected, he cocked an eyebrow. "Say what?"

"EVPs," I repeated, "Electronic Voice Phenomenon. Basically, they're sounds captured by a recording device not detected by the human ear. Some claim they're proof of paranormal activity." I paused and considered the idea. "While others insist they're nothing more than delusions and audio glitches."

"Oh yeah?" Ralph replied with more than a hint of sarcasm. "Messages from ghosts on your TV, home stereo, or one of those friggin' iPods all those snotty kids seem to have attached to their heads?"

"That's basically it," I summarized.

"Bunch of bullshit that is." Ralph snorted. "You know what you said about delusions?"

I nodded, waiting for the driver's inevitable conclusion.

"I'm gonna go with that." Ralph steered the taxi around a corner foregoing the use of the breaks. Not paying attention to the squealing tires, he locked eyes with me in the mirror. "What do you think, buddy?"

I wasn't convinced either way, but it had been something that captured my imagination. For better or worse. "Not sure."

"I'll tell you what I think," he stated as if I had a choice in the matter. "Buncha whacko, nut jobs with too much time on their hands making this stupid shit up. Probably writers with overactive imaginations." He paused just long enough to swerve manically through traffic. "So, what do you do, buddy?"

I laughed. "I'm one of those writers with overactive imaginations."

"No shit?" As Ralph swerved through the street, he placed his arm on the back of the seat and peered over his shoulder at me. "What's your name?"

"Jack Devlin," I said, emphatically pointing toward the windshield as it rapidly filled with red lights.

"I'll be damned," the cabbie answered and returned his eyes forward. Slamming on the breaks, he brought the taxi to a screeching halt. Without missing a beat, he turned back to me. "I read Five 'Til Midnight. Helluva good book."

I tried to respond, but my tongue was still firmly lodged in my throat and I was certain I was as white as a ghost.

"Hey, tell me something," Ralph said as the car started to creep forward. "I heard you were investigated by the FBI because you wrote about assassinating the President. Is that true?"

Finally able to draw breath, I loosened my tongue from the roof of my mouth. "Actually," I said, then swallowed, "it is. Because of 9/11, the FBI treated my assassination scenario very seriously. I was questioned, but fortunately, nothing really ever came of it."

Ralph smiled and pulled back into traffic as the light changed to green. "Do any of the Feds you met look like those two from that show about aliens?"

"Aliens?" I searched my brain's databanks for FBI plus aliens. "Oh, you mean Agents Mulder and Scully from The X-Files?"

Ralph snapped his fingers. "That's them. Did you meet a looker like that Scully girl?"

"'Fraid not," I answered sadly. "Just run-of-the-mill government agents."

"That's too bad." Ralph laughed hoarsely as if he had just smoked three packs straight. "She's a Betty. I'd let her investigate me anytime, if you know what I mean." He laughed again and slapped the steering wheel.

I shook my head trying to understand how our conversation had wound from EVPs, to my books, and now crude sexual innuendo about Gillian Anderson.

The heavyset cabbie coughed as he tried to catch his breath. Rubbing a bit of spittle off his bottom lip, he created a sound I was sure was a screaming slug being crushed in his windpipe. Patting his chest with a solid thump, he returned his attention to the rearview mirror. "Is it true your wife killed herself?"

I felt a quick stab of pain in my chest, then the inevitable pang of nausea. Reeling in my seat, a floodgate of emotions was unleashed. An instant, powerful depression hit me as her face appeared in my memory, then anger as I saw blood...it was everywhere. I turned and looked helplessly out the cab's window. "I'd rather not talk about it."

"Oh," the insensitive clod exhaled, realizing he had unintentionally wounded me. "Say no more. Shouldn't have brought it up."

That was more of an apology than I got from most people who broached the subject. "Don't worry about it," I said after a moment, finally able to gain control of my emotions. "You didn't know."

"Thanks," the heavyset man answered. He glanced up at a street corner sign. "Almost there. You can see The Hollow now." He lifted a finger from the steering wheel and pointed.

I lifted my gaze to the front windshield.

Amidst a cave of trees, the dark-gray home rose like a phantom beyond the horizon. Two stories with a huge attic, the house was tall and slender. The first floor spread out like wings at the base and a heavy, iron fence encased and protected it. White-framed windows were spread across the façade, while the jet-black front door stood over a large, rounded staircase that looked like the house's bottom lip. Barren of leaves, massive, gnarled trees in the front yard reached up with bony fingers, appearing like skeletal disciples worshipping the beast. The snow and ice that clung to the dark roof only made it seem more foreboding.

I fought against the urge to tell Ralph to stop and turn around. As I stared at The Hollow, dread started to ball and sat like a rock in my belly. "Are you sure that's the right place?"

Ralph nodded. "Sure as rain."

Sure as rain? Wasn't the expression "right as rain"? And what the hell does that colorful little

14

euphemism even mean? It sounds so…dumb.

I started to stow my laptop nervously as we approached. I had to do something to keep my eyes away from the house.

"I'll have you there in a second," Ralph reported from the captain's chair. "Hey," he added sheepishly, "is there any way I can get you to autograph a novel for me?"

I took a breath in through my nose and considered the request. "Yeah, sure. Let me have it," I said, digging a pen out of my laptop bag.

"I don't actually have one," Ralph said a bit embarrassed.

Turning the wheel slowly, the cabbie maneuvered the car off the road and onto the front drive. Passing through the open iron gates, the house loomed above us.

"Then what am I supposed to sign?" I held up my hands so he wouldn't even attempt to answer. I already understood. Digging into my laptop bag on the seat next to me, I found a copy of my latest novel, Jessie's Warning. Flipping open the cover, I held my pen to the page. "Who do I make this out to?"

Ralph stared at me for a moment as he brought the car to a halt in front of The Hollow. "Um, eBay?"

Would anyone miss him if I reached over the seat and strangled him?

Chapter Two

Alone, I reeled as it took my senses a moment to process the wealth of stimuli. My eyes, still affected from the bright winter sun, slowly adjusted to the dim levels of light inside the house. Rich oak wood stretched along the walls, but it didn't feel as I would have expected. Instead, the house felt cold and uninviting. Undeterred, I adjusted my laptop bag on my shoulder and moved further inside. Scanning the foyer, I caught a fleeting glimpse of movement in my peripheral vision that made the hairs on my arms stand up. My pulse raced as I snapped my head around. Trying not to blink, I pulled a breath into my lungs and held it. I focused on a spot in the foyer and waited.

"Jack?"

Ripped from the moment, I spun as though intoxicated, nearly spilling to the ground. My hand reached out instinctively and braced against the nearest wall as I tried to calm my heart flipping and flopping in my chest.

A woman, in a terrible mustard yellow jacket, stood inside the entrance. "Oof da!" she bellowed with a definite Minnesota accent. Moving to my side, she placed her hand on my shoulder as a deep look of concern on her face. "Are you okay?"

I took a breath and flashed my most charming smile hoping I didn't look like a lunatic. "You just scared me. I'm fine."

"You don't look fine." Her worry had not abated, even in the face of my suave assurances.

"You look like you've seen a ghost."

I laughed, despite her comment. "I'm okay. Just a little jet lagged I guess."

"Okay," she breathed finally. Extending her hand with a business card, she put on her best smile. "I'm Cynthia Glass, by the way. The agency sent me to give you a tour of The Hollow."

I accepted the card and shook the woman's hand. "Nice to meet you."

Cynthia was probably five years younger than me, but in her oversized gold realtor jacket, she looked like a child who had been playing in her parents' closet. Her nametag, nothing more than a rectangular hunk of plastic with an ugly sticker attached, hung crooked on her lapel. Her plain black skirt just passed the hem of her jacket but showed off her slender legs. Her short, mousy-brown hair was pulled up behind her head with a few loose strands framing her pretty face. I say "pretty," because she wasn't exactly horrible to look at, but she wasn't gorgeous either. She had that girl-next-door vibe, which in itself wasn't a terrible thing. She was one of those people who instantly became your long-lost, best friend, no matter if you wanted her to or not. She was a real estate agent, but somewhere in her syrupy, sugar-coated brain, that equated to instant friendship. I suppose it could all have been part of her sales technique, or possibly a genetic defect. I wasn't entirely certain which. Still, she was more pleasant than most of the realtors I had worked with.

My eyes wandered up and around the foyer. "Why is it called The Hollow?"

"Interesting story," she said like a tour guide who had just been given her segue. "The gentleman who built it, Lincoln Ezekiel, was actually one of the first mayors of Union. He was shot dead here in 1799 in a dispute over a parcel of land. The killer was never apprehended. Ezekiel named it The Hollow after one of his favorite stories as a child."

"The Legend of Sleepy Hollow," I guessed, although I was sure it was correct.

Cynthia nodded. "By Washington Irving."

I looked around the foyer expectantly.

"So," Cynthia said after a long moment, the silence apparently bothering her. "You never told me, what brings you to Union?"

"Meeting with my editor in New York," I answered without really considering the question. My thoughts were elsewhere. But that wasn't the only reason I was in this tiny suburb of New York. I had been doing research for almost a year now, and somehow heard of The Hollow via an Internet forum. Then the stars seemed to have aligned and brought me here. The thought made me strangely uncomfortable.

"So you're a writer?" Cynthia had that same glazed look in her eyes I had when people talked about their kids. "What do you write about?"

"All of those things that go bump in the night," I said mischievously.

"I don't like horror," the young realtor admitted. "I prefer romance."

"I never would have guessed," I said sarcastically, giving her the stink eye. It was time to change the subject. "Tell me about the house."

Cynthia nodded eagerly, but clearly didn't comprehend my thinly veiled unhappiness. "This home was originally built in 1792, thought it was rebuilt in 1957 after being damaged by fire. It has subsequently been modified several times, so very little of the original structure remains." She stepped back and spread her arms out like a ringmaster while she continued to describe the house. She had just busted out her "A" game and was enthusiastically showing me the elephants, clowns, and dancing monkeys. I followed her out of the foyer into the family room.

It spilled around us with rich hardwood floors and heavy red walls as far as the eye could see. The room's roughly octagonal shape and dark colors tried to hide its size, but failed. A dark rug woven with various shades of brown and black stretched across the floor with a single matching sofa in the center. A few framed prints occupied space on the walls, while a sparse smattering of ferns lived in the corners. It seemed lifeless and even though it was probably my imagination, it seemed a few degrees cooler than the entrance. As a knot began to ball in my stomach, my feet pushed me uneasily out of the room. I didn't feel as though I belonged here.

Cynthia stopped her sales pitch in mid-sell. "You don't look so well."

She started to reach for me but I sidestepped her and lifted my arms to guard against another intrusion into my telephone booth of personal space. I felt the skin on my arms crawl. "You know," I breathed, realizing she had just provided my escape route, "I think you're right. I'm suddenly feeling a bit under the weather. Can we continue this some other time?"

Cynthia nodded. "Certainly, Jack. I just hope you feel better. Can I call someone to come get you?"

"No." I shook my head. "I think I just need some rest. I'm going to head back to my hotel room."

"All right," Cynthia finally agreed as if she were my mother deciding if I was worthy of the car keys for the evening. "Call me when you feel better." She started to reach for me, but stopped. "The house will be here when you're ready."

The comment struck me oddly. "What does that mean?"

"You're the only one who's seen the house in months," Cynthia answered. "Seems the housing bubble finally burst."

I didn't buy it. The house was beautifully maintained with five bedrooms, two floors, huge basement, attic space, and the asking price was extremely low. Why hadn't anyone snapped it up yet? My mind began to whirl stopping on the obvious question: What's wrong with it, other than perhaps being haunted?

"Thank you, Cynthia," I finally conceded.

Turning away from the octagonal room, I proceeded to traverse the foyer and grabbed the door handle. As if a charge of electricity went through me, I instantly stiffened. Someone was watching me, but it wasn't Cynthia. I felt a pair of eyes settle on my back, burning into me like lasers. My instincts told me to charge out the door and not look back, but curiosity was overwhelming me. I cautiously fought my flight reflex and looked over my shoulder.

Nothing.

My eyes followed a red rug that crept up a wide, lazy staircase in the back of the foyer until I reached the top landing. Despite the presence of a large window, there seemed to be a heavy shadow. It clung defiantly to the floor, walls, and railing defying the light that spilled in through the dirty panes of glass. A chill ran down the back of my neck and into my stomach as I stared.

I couldn't be absolutely certain, but I swore at that moment, the shadow shifted.

Before I realized what my body was doing, I was out the door, off the front porch, down the stairs and into the snow-covered front lawn. I spun and looked back in through the open door only to see Cynthia moving toward me, clearly panicked.

Had she seen something too?

As my lungs pumped gulps of air in and out, I tried to collect my scattered thoughts.

"Jack," Cynthia said as she waded into the snow after me. Wearing only pumps, I was fairly certain she was going to regret it. Ignoring my attempts to push her away, she grabbed onto my shoulders. Her eyes were wide. "What's wrong?"

"Did you...?" I let the question die before it could fully take form. She already thought I was crazy, best not to add more to the list.

"Did I what?" She waited patiently for the culmination of the thought. "Jack?"

Forcefully pulling my eyes away from the front

door, they settled on Cynthia. Swallowing another breath of air, I finally regained some of my composure. "Did you," I stalled, grasping for any thought that didn't end with ghost, "give me your business card?"

Cynthia looked dumbfounded for a moment, but quickly recovered—much faster than I did actually. "I thought I did." She reached into her oversized jacket pocket and produced a small stack of cards. "Here's another. My office and cell numbers are listed so you can contact me anytime to reschedule."

I nodded and started to trudge out of the snow. "I appreciate this," I added as an afterthought.

Glancing over my shoulder one final time, my eyes quickly darted from Cynthia and were drawn back to the still open front door of the house. I was undeniably curious. The stories were apparently true about this place.

I was certain my search had just ended.

Chapter Three

I had intended to head back to my hotel, but a small, warm diner invited me in. The wind had picked up as the sun sank into the west and simply propping up the collar of my jacket wasn't cutting it. I would have taken a taxi or let Cynthia drive me home, but after today I needed time to process. I may have actually found what I was looking for. I had been working toward this for so long it was almost unimaginable it had actually arrived.

Sliding into an empty booth, the green vinyl seat squeaked announcing my arrival. Looking like something straight out of the fifties, I could imagine cute sweatered couples sitting at the long bar in the center jointly sipping a malt. I wondered for a moment if kids from that period had actually ever done that or if it was just another Hollywood fabrication. I let the idea escape. Beige, white, and mint green were the overriding colors while silver accents kept them separate. Numerous neon signs littered the walls advertising everything from their world famous hot dogs, to a cool, refreshing glass of cherry cola.

Glancing around, I watched curious pairs of eyes shrink away as I met their gaze.

Sliding a bit further down into the padded bench, I stuffed my hands into my pockets and let my eyes fall to the more-or-less white table. Battle scars from thousands of meals delivered and demolished marred the surface. A deep gouge, slicing from the outer edge and terminating before the salt and pepper, looked more like the aftermath of a plane crash than something a knife or fork could cause. The seats appeared almost camouflaged with their numerous ground-in stains, while the foamy yellow innards bled defiantly through duct tape sutures. It didn't entirely scream "clean," but what greasy spoon did? Still, it had character and that was what mattered. Try and tell that to the health department though.

"Need to see a menu?"

I glanced up at a full-figured waitress with wiry dark hair she had attempted to pull into a ponytail. Strands of her messy hair shot out in all directions despite the effort she had taken to tame it. A waitress uniform that matched the green of the diner, and a white apron was wrapped around her body like too little Saran wrap on a half-eaten slab of beef.

I cringed at the analogy. My mind gets a little too descriptive from time to time and I often regret it. I'd have to remind myself to delete that one from my databanks later. "I'd just like a cheeseburger and a cup of coffee."

Her eyes were deep-set and oozed discontent. It was obvious life had taken great pains to beat her down. She jotted notes hastily on her thin white notepad then deposited her pen behind her ear, which immediately vanished in the living monster that was her hair. Without blinking, she turned back toward the kitchen. I decided she wasn't human after all, rather some poorly-built automaton created by a desperate diner owner so he wouldn't have to hire a real person. Somewhere in the creation

24

process, her mold had been severely damaged by grease from the deep fryer and her programming was compromised when lettuce was substituted for her neural network. At least I hoped to God that was the case. I couldn't imagine a real person looking that utterly and completely miserable.

"Jack Devlin?"

I turned at the sound of my name, silently hoping there was another Jack Devlin in the diner. To my dismay, there wasn't.

A thin blonde walked toward me. Her blond hair was dulling as dark roots overtook it. A t-shirt, much too short for her stomach's physical condition, stretched over her chest while a fashionably distressed pair of jeans covered her legs. A thick, pink coat with a fuzzy collar completed the ensemble. It was almost more than I could take.

I looked up at the blond patiently hoping beyond hope to be struck down by a rogue shark attack. "Yes?" The word clawed and bit my tongue so as not to be released.

The blonde's eyes widened. "I'm a big fan!"

Oh lord.

Without asking, my perky fan seated herself opposite me. "I just finished Jessie's Warning," she announced, "and I loved it! It scared the hell out of me, and the surprise ending was amazing."

If she reached for me, I was going to bolt. "Thank you," I breathed. Maybe now that she had said her bit she would leave.

"Where did you come up with the idea for Jessie?"

Nope.

I sighed but bit my tongue. I didn't want the company right now, but I couldn't turn away a paying fan either. It was time to bust out the stock reply. "Jessie, like most of my characters, is a composite of many of the people I've encountered in my life, added to a healthy dose of imagination. Her particular personality was custom tailored for the story." It was the same answer I'd given a thousand times for all of my books, only the character's name changed. And apparently, she was buying it.

The blonde's eyes washed over with joy. "That's so amazing," she breathed. "Each time I read one of your novels, your creativity amazes me. How one mind can come up with so many different characters and stories is absolutely incredible!" She squirmed exuberantly in her seat. "Every time I read one of your novels, I feel like you're writing exclusively for me."

I had a Kathy Bates/Misery flash. Certain the color had just drained from my face, my brain tried to cover the discomfort. "Uh, thank you, Mrs....?"

"Miss," the blonde corrected seductively. "Ms. Amy Allen."

And she was single, too. I hung my head. I had just acquired a new stalker. "It's nice to meet you. You live here in Union?"

Amy nodded. "Unfortunately, born and bred. Still, it's not too far from New York." She stopped and seemed extremely sad for a moment, as if she had just realized a great tragedy. Slowly, she brought her soft blue eyes back up to meet mine.

26

"What's a famous author like you doing here though?"

I didn't want to say I was in the process of moving here for fear she would find my house and I would come home one day and discover her standing naked in my living room covered in my dog's blood… "Research," I blurted out.

"A new novel," Amy asked excitedly, "about Union, New York?"

I smiled. "I'm not at liberty to discuss that."

"Ah," she breathed, winked, and tapped her nose slyly. "Of course. Say no more." She leaned across the table exposing her cleavage and lowered her voice to sound as sexy as possible. "But should there be a spunky blonde in the story, I would be happy to let you study me."

Study her? What did that even mean? Then it hit me. I felt instantly embarrassed at such a shameless come on…but I had to say something. "I'll keep that in mind, Amy."

Seemingly delighted that I had spoken her name, Amy writhed pleasurably in her seat for a moment. Finally regaining her composure, she slid off the edge of the seat and stood. Running her fingers over the tabletop as if she were caressing her lover's face, she dropped one final smoldering glance on me before taking a step back. Turning as gracefully as possible, Amy swaggered away shaking her hips.

Finding a fan who was completely turned on by my imagination wasn't odd. Finding one like Amy, who was a little "spooky," was. Authors didn't usually have sex-starved groupies. Still, if I wasn't who I was, I might consider her offer to "study." That wasn't me though.

The smack of a plate against the table ripped me back to reality. Spinning with a start, my eyes quickly ramped up from the disheveled cheeseburger to the hollow-eyed waitress whose hand was still pulling away from the plate. "Was that absolutely necessary?"

The waitress shrugged and turned away. "Enjoy," she added in what felt more like a warning than anything else.

"Customer service is dead," I remarked, "just like your tip."

The waitress spun on her heels and glared angrily at me as if I had just threatened her with bodily harm. Her eyes wandered down to my meal then back up to me. I knew she was deciding whether to kick me out or lean over, lift my top bun, and spit directly on my hamburger.

But I didn't care.

I had come to the point in my life where I no longer tolerated poor service. Every industry that revolved around customer service had shriveled up and died in my opinion. I never, ever tipped on a percentage of the bill, but rather the quality of service. Let it be known that I am a generous tipper when the situation calls for it, but I had also been known for leaving a strongly worded note on the state of customer service in lieu of a gratuity.

Her eyes finally, thankfully, fell away from me. Gritting her teeth, the waitress straightened her stained apron and marched back toward the kitchen without a single word. I'm not sure if she had simply given up and accepted that she had rendered bad service, or some other reason I couldn't possibly fathom, but her eyes seemed even more hollow than before.

Turning my attention back to my meal, I realized my appetite was waning. Plus, I had no idea what had been done to my cheeseburger outside of my presence. I didn't feel as if I wanted to risk it. Glancing up at the kitchen, I spotted a scruffy, haggard chef staring intently at me through the rectangular pick-up window. As our eyes met, he quickly shrank away and disappeared. I was absolutely certain I wasn't eating now.

Sliding out of the booth, I dug into my pant pocket and produced a wad of bills. I wasn't sure why I was paying for my meal when I didn't eat a bite, or even get my cup of coffee, but never let it be said that Jack Devlin skipped out on a bill. Digging a ten out of the pack, I dropped it on the table and headed back for the door. I guess it was back to the hotel after all. Maybe I could order room service.

Chapter Four

"I feel like I'm losing myself."

The words spilled from her mouth and pooled on the counter, threatening to consume me. It sounded innocent enough, but the statement was acidic, venomous, and rife with anger and hatred. I recoiled almost instinctively, as my heart dropped with a dull plop into my stomach. I stared in awe at my wife trying to comprehend the declaration. Her beautiful brown eyes seemed almost black in the low light, and her usually wavy hair fell flat from her head. Her skin, usually smooth and vibrant, appeared dull and lifeless. Dark bags were forming under her eyes, and Irene looked absolutely exhausted. I couldn't remember a time when she appeared so bereft of life.

"How can you say that?" It was the only response I could form.

"I used to be so much," she dropped her gaze to the equally lifeless plate of pasta before her and used her fork to pick at it, "more. Do you remember when I used to go out dancing with friends?" Irene lifted her gaze to meet mine, her eyes brimming with tears she refused to let loose.

I shook my head vehemently. "I never stopped you from—"

"I used to paint," she continued despite my interruption. "I used to have my own dreams." She dropped her fork on the porcelain plate with an angry clank. "Not just yours."

I didn't respond. I didn't know what to say. I let

my eyes wander to the window and the red and gold landscape of Southern Idaho in the fall. It was beautiful, and somehow completely disconnected from the pain and anger that hovered around me in the kitchen.

Her bottom lip quivered. "Remember when I was more than just Mrs. Jack Devlin?"

It was a verbal punch to the gut.

"Don't get me wrong," she backtracked suddenly, "I do love you, Jack. I just can't be the Stepford Wife you want." Irene stood from her stool and charged out of the kitchen.

Her withdrawal was unexpected, and infuriating. Pulling the hand towel off my shoulder, I tossed it on the counter and snapped off the burners below the dinner I had prepared. I shouldn't have chased her. That was mistake number one.

"Wait!" I shouted as I moved from behind the kitchen counter and followed her. "How can you say that to me and then walk away?" I was asking the question before I even made it into the living room.

Irene was perched on the edge of the couch with her face buried in her hands.

Her pain didn't deter me. "Don't I take care of you? Doesn't being Mrs. Jack Devlin afford you everything you want?"

I heard her sob.

Admittedly, I had just kicked her, but I was angry and feeling a little underappreciated. That was mistake number two. "You can't just drop something like that on me in the middle of dinner then dash off."

31

"Why do you even care?" Irene looked up at me with black mascara tears running down her cheeks. "All you do is sit in your damned office, write your stupid stories, and ignore me."

My eyes hardened in anger. "This," I threw my arms out gesturing to everything around us, "is what my stupid stories gave us. How dare you insult my work?"

"Work?" she scoffed. "Is that what you call it?"

"It's my job," I defended myself, "and it affords us a very, very good life." What was wrong with her? She had never attacked my writing before.

She choked back a sob and tried to wipe the tears from her face, but only succeeded in smearing her mascara further. "What about me?"

I shrugged, obviously missing her point. "What about you?"

"Where do I fit in?" Irene ran the back of her hand under her nose. She was falling apart right before my eyes. "What do I do? Am I just supposed to cater to your whims when you want me? Screw when you want to? Then just hide in the corner until you need me again? Is that all that I am?"

Her rage was undeniable. The flames of anger leapt off her threatening to scorch me. "Irene," I breathed, sensing I was losing a battle I had no idea I was even embroiled in.

She jumped up from her perch and charged me. "Who am I, Jack?"

I didn't understand the question.

She slammed the heel of her hand into my chest with a force that surprised me. "Tell me who I am! Who am I, Jack?"

"Irene Devlin, my wife," I replied, unsure of what answer she wanted. And that was my third, and final, mistake.

"Exactly," Irene whispered and shrank away from me. Tears rolled down her beautiful face leaving pain-filled trails of makeup. Looking up, she breathed out slowly trying to somehow compose herself. Sobbing again, she turned and walked slowly out of the living room.

I was absolutely stunned.

I should have followed her. I should have taken her into my arms, even if she didn't want to be held. I should have told her that everything was going to be all right. I should have explained that she was the light of my life, and how I would do anything she wanted me to. I should have done something.

But I didn't.

I rolled onto my side and stared at the display on the hotel's alarm clock. The red numbers were casting an evil glare across the nightstand and spilling through my nearly empty glass of scotch. Nearing three in the morning, I had been asleep for several hours, yet it only felt like moments. I couldn't escape the pain of the repeated dream, nor could I remember a night when I hadn't relived it in my mind's eye. It was haunting me. She was haunting me.

And I was letting her.

Propping myself up on my elbow, I swung my legs over the edge of the bed and slowly sat up. I pulled my hands across my face then looked over my room. Sufficiently lavish, the bedroom was separate from a mini-kitchen, while the bathroom, a magnificent, marbled bastion that would have made Caesar envious, was complete with bath, shower, and spa. A large living room was directly off the kitchen with a small table near the floor-to-ceiling window, and two couches arranged the only way they could be. A single nineteen-inch television occupied the far wall atop a waist-high entertainment center. I didn't need any of it though, but it was still nice to have. It made me feel more important than I actually was.

After spending roughly ten minutes trying to access the hotel's advertised free wireless high-speed connection and failing, I decided email was overrated and raided the minibar for a stiff drink. Ah, there it was, buried behind the overpriced bags of peanuts and the family friendly juices: my old friend Vodka. I pulled the bottle from the bar and stared at the clear liquor inside. Vodka and I had spent a lot of time together. We had developed a love/hate relationship. Basically, I loved to hate it. Approximately the same size as those served on flights, I snatched out the three remaining bottles and set them on the counter. Eyeballing one of the water glasses with what was certainly a state-of-the-art paper cap half falling off, I decided to drink straight out of the bottle. I could kill myself just fine that way without having to worry about E Coli.

After scooping the bottles into my arms, I trekked across the thick carpet and plopped down on one of the two beige love seats. Arranging the bottles in a row on the knee-high coffee table in front of me, I couldn't help but note how they looked like soldiers standing at attention. Cracking open the first soldier's head, I tipped it back to my lips and took a quick swallow. With a flavor somewhere between rotgut vodka and rubbing alcohol, the heady substance burned as it rolled down my throat. I gulped down the rest of the bottle and set it back by its comrades. As the burning passed, I felt warmth spread into my stomach. It tasted terrible, but it was better than a sharp stick in the eye. Although, not by much.

My mind wandered back to The Hollow and the dark form at the top of the stairs. Had I really seen it, or imagined the whole thing…? Even though it had happened only hours earlier, it felt like a distant, hazy memory. I tried to recall details about the scene, and though I had stared right at it, I couldn't remember any specific details about the darkness. Perhaps I was simply overtired and my mind was playing tricks on me, but it all seemed so real. I rubbed the bridge of my nose. Had it come to the point where I couldn't even trust my own senses? I know it happened.

Leaning back, I stared at my laptop sitting quietly on the opposite couch. It was beckoning to me. I had heard its siren song many times before, only to have my hopes dashed. It wanted me to write. As the multicolored screen saver banged and flickered about the black screen, it said to me, "C'mon, Jack, it's easy. Just put your hands on the keyboard. We can make beautiful prose together." I turned my attention back to the bottles on the table, but I could feel it eyeing me. It wasn't going to take no for an answer, but I knew what would happen. As soon as I took it into my lap and gently placed my fingers on its smooth, convex, laser-etched keys, it would laugh and mock me while I stared at a blank page. It was secretly evil, though disguised in saintly white. I should fling it off the balcony. That would prove who's the boss in this relationship.

Snapping off another soldier's helmet, I tossed it back. It occurred to me that I didn't want to go to bed, even though I knew I would regret this, instead I wanted to head down to the hotel bar. At least in the bar I had the chance of getting drunk with someone. There was nothing worse in my book than getting drunk alone. Drunkenness was a social function. It really didn't serve any other purpose as far as I'm concerned. The idea of getting blitzed then throwing up alone really doesn't hold much appeal to me.

Maybe I'm just odd that way.

Standing, I felt the alcohol work into the rest of my body. It wasn't enough to get me drunk, but I could at least feel it. After walking back into the bedroom, I dropped down on the edge of my queen-sized bed and rounded up my shoes. I usually preferred sneakers, but since this was a business trip, I had broken out my good black leather shoes. Pulling them onto my tired feet, I felt a twinge of pain in my temple as though someone had just stabbed an ice pick into my brain. I wondered for a moment if it was the alcohol. Sitting up quickly, I took a slow breath as it subsided.

Wandering into the massive, cathedral-like bathroom, I stopped in front of the sink and leaned over. After twisting on the hot tap, I splashed warm water on my face. Running my wet hands through my hair, I felt a thick strand fall down over my forehead. Resting my palms on the white porcelain basin, I looked up into the wide bank of mirrors. I was going to turn forty in November, an age that scared the hell out of me, and it was finally starting to show on my face. My dark brown hair used to be wavy and full of body, but now hung almost straight down to my collar, and my blue eyes, which I recall looking vibrant, appeared dulled like melting ice. Crow's feet stretched out from the corners of them, like a roadmap of my life etched in flesh. It wasn't that I had a hard life—I certainly hadn't spent my life digging ditches or mining coal—it's just that I lived my life to the fullest when I was younger. Now it seemed my wild hedonism and youthful indiscretions were catching up with me.

My reflection looked hollow. I was empty. I suppose it happens to all writers. There comes a point at which there is no more pain to channel onto the page, no more hurt from your past that longs to be dealt with. We are merely vessels after all, and there is no such thing as a bottomless cup. I'm thirty-nine and have been writing for most of my life, professionally for the past eleven years. Every nook and cranny of my soul has been exposed to the light and fully explored. In my writing, I find those things that scare the hell out of me, like personal tragedies, losses, and pain, then stamp them with black ink for the entire world to see. Of course, I deceptively disguise the problems as those of my characters, so no one truly knows it's really my psychosis. I had given all that I could. Yet, they wanted more.

I didn't know if I had anything left to offer.

Turning away from my depressing reflection, I snatched a towel off the marble—or faux marble, I couldn't tell—countertop and wiped my face. Tossing it onto the floor, I then wandered back into my bedroom and snatched my black leather blazer out of the closet. I had eschewed my comfort clothes in favor of a pair of khakis and a black button-up shirt as my trip to Union had called for more, let's call it "professional" attire.

Snatching my keys off the nightstand, I started toward the door. I had to be at my editor's office in less than eight hours. I knew I should get some sleep, but I had been living with the dead for so long I craved human companionship. Pulling open the door, I glanced one final time back into my room. Gulping down a breath of air, I shut the door and headed for the lobby.

Chapter Five

The lobby bar was pretty much as I imagined it would be at three in the morning: nearly empty. A lone barkeep held his post at the bar reading the help wanted ads, while the only waitress on duty sprawled out on a nearby table fast asleep. A thin smattering of patrons nursed their drinks and looked as though they were waiting for something. The sole customer at the bar, a heavyset Hispanic woman in a dark shawl, was slowly peeling the label from her beer bottle. The sheer beauty of this iconic moment wasn't lost on me. The only thing missing was a lonely piano player spilling the blues in the corner.

As if on cue, dulcet piano tones rose up from nowhere and wafted through the bar. Ahhh...it was perfect now.

Spinning slowly, I spotted the piano on a slightly raised stage. Situated directly opposite the bar, the musician was partially obscured by his instrument. I could see the edges of a wrinkled gray suit, a dark blue tie hanging limply from his undone collar, and a fedora slung back lazily over his wavy brown hair. A single cigarette smoldered in a glass ashtray on the top of the piano. The bluish-gray smoke wound down around the piano player like the hands of some unseen lover caressing his face.

I couldn't see his fingers working the ivories, but the look of sheer emotional anguish on his face told me that he wasn't merely playing the blues, but living them. His melody was slow and winding as it dipped pain and loss, yet there were brief moments of respite where the listener almost felt as if they could be redeemed. But they were fleeting as the notes shuffled the listener back onto the musical rollercoaster.

No one in the bar seemed to be paying attention to the music, save for me. I'm sure these were the regulars, so this was probably nothing new. As the man finished his song on a minor chord, he plucked his cigarette from its perch and took a heady drag. Holding it in his lungs for a moment, he finally exhaled. After another drag, he returned the coffin nail to the ashtray and rested his fingers on the keys again. As the song began I turned and walked toward the bar.

Placing my hands on the bar's glossy veneer, my eyes were drawn to the deep, rich wood beneath. I watched it move like a river from one side to the other, the lines in the grain winding and twisting as they went. Pulling my fingertips gently back to the gold handrail, I looked up to meet the expectant gaze of the bartender. In his early thirties, his frame was average with a bit extra here and there, but he still looked good in the crisp black and white uniform he wore. A black vest was wrapped over his perfectly white dress shirt and blended perfectly into his slacks. His slender tie, knotted at his throat, disappeared behind the vest, while his sleeves were tastefully rolled up exposing his muscular forearms and a fading tattoo. His hair, jet black and curly, melded into his thin, perfectly kept beard. His face was masculine and strong, and looked somehow familiar. I couldn't place him though.

"What'll you have?" came the inevitable

question from the barkeep's deep, milky voice.

"Vodka," I said as I slid onto the nearest stool.

With a nod, the bartender folded his classifieds and stuffed them into an unseen cubby behind the bar. With a snap of his fingers, he repeated my order and snatched a tall bottle of alcohol from the rack behind him.

Glancing down the bar, I locked eyes with the Hispanic woman in the dark shawl as she stared intently at me. I let my gaze drop quickly. Crossing my arms, I leaned forward on the rail.

The bartender set a glass on the bar before me. "So what brings you in tonight?"

"Couldn't sleep," I offered. I peered over my shoulder at the waitress still asleep on the table. "Is it always this busy in here?"

"Oh yeah," the bartender said dryly as he poured the clear alcohol. "Have to beat the customers away with a stick."

I nodded with a half-smile as I understood why he was reading the classifieds. "How long have you been here?"

"A little over six months," the bartender answered as he completed my order. "This is only a part-time gig until I get back on my feet."

I cocked my head inquisitively. As a writer, I loved hearing stories. They had a unique way of getting into my brain, mixing with my own experiences, and creating interesting characters for my novels. There was nothing better than a touch of realism, especially in the horror genre, to connect the reader. "Do you mind if I ask what happened to knock you off your feet?"

The bartender shrugged. "Divorce. She got everything."

I nodded. "Isn't that always the way?"

"Yeah." He sighed. "She basically took my life away. So, after my regular full-time job, here I am in this monkey suit for four or five hours a night slinging drinks to drunken businessmen." His eyes fell on me as he realized what he had said. "No offense."

I waved off his concern. "None taken."

"I used to be an architect," the bartender admitted. He stopped and lost himself in thought for a moment. "You know the new war memorial they're building downtown? The one for the soldiers lost in Desert Storm?"

I nodded. "Yeah, I think I read something about that. Why?"

"I designed it." The bartender pointed his thumb to his chest. "Six months of blood, sweat, and tears and I had it all taken away."

I snapped my fingers. "I knew I recognized you! I read that interview with you in Time Magazine. Your name is," I paused rolling around the letter R in my mouth, "Robert?"

The bartender nodded and extended his hand. "Robert Lang," he acknowledged. "My wife's father was my partner at the firm. When Janie bailed on me, she took him with her. So," Robert breathed, "here I am working two jobs trying to gather enough capital to start my own firm. I should have the doors open by oh," he paused and glanced playfully at his watch, "the first of never."

"Well." I snickered but quickly tried to hide it.

"At least you have a plan." I reached down and snatched my drink off the bar. Tilting it back to my lips I felt the alcohol slide down my throat. It burned like lighter fluid and tasted almost as bad. Gritting my teeth and balling my fist, I forcefully choked it down. Apparently this bar didn't understand the concept of buying top shelf. I looked up at Robert with watery eyes and a frog in my throat. "That's smooth."

Robert nodded enjoying my moment of discomfort for laughing at him. I suppose—in retrospect—I would have done the same thing.

As the acidic burn in my throat finally began to ease, I pulled in a breath and wiped the tears from my eyes. Pushing the glass of turpentine away, I sat up and became aware the piano music had stopped. Spinning on my barstool, I peered over my shoulder toward the piano. The musician was gone. I turned back to Robert with a slightly perplexed look on my face. "Did the piano player finish his set already? He was only on his second song."

"Second song?" Robert grabbed my glass of faux vodka and quickly dumped it, perhaps considering he had poisoned me and was disposing of the evidence. "The piano player's off tonight."

"But I just saw a man sitting there playing the blues." I stared at the empty piano incredulously. I knew what I had seen and heard. "He was wearing a gray suit, blue tie, and a fedora. He was smoking a cigarette." I sniffed the air but couldn't detect the lingering hint of smoke. I stood from my stool.

"Sir," Robert said, then let out a sigh, "there's no piano player on tonight and this is a nonsmoking establishment."

Had I imagined the whole thing? I knew I was tired, but to make up the whole thing in my head? Shaking my head, I turned and walked briskly to the piano. Stepping up to the stage, my hands hit the top of the piano and I stopped. The ashtray was still there, but there was no trace of usage. There were no ashes, and no butts.

After sliding around the keyboard, I slumped onto the bench and stared. My hands fell uselessly in my lap.

"Told you," was Robert's reply from across the bar.

Ignoring the has-been bartender, I continued to stare at the piano. I could see the player in my mind's eye, sitting exactly where I was. He was here...I knew it for certain. I could see his wavy brown hair peeking out from beneath his fedora, the wrinkles on the lapels of his suit jacket, and the sheen from his silk tie in the low light. I could remember him perfectly, except his face. It occurred to me then I had no idea what he physically looked like. I could describe his clothes, his hair, the brand of cigarette he smoked and the style of music he played, but I couldn't remember a single detail of his face. No eye color, no idea if he had a mustache or beard. I had no idea.

Standing up from the piano, I jumped to the edge of the stage. "Excuse me," I addressed the entire bar and waited. No one moved. I clapped my hands loudly. "Excuse me!"

Glazed and drunken eyes lifted up from their glasses of poison and settled on me.

44

"Thank you," I said, trying to remember my speech classes from high school and project my voice. "Quick question, how many of you saw the piano player up here?"

All the hands in the bar slowly raised into the air.

My confidence was building, but it quickly died as I realized who I was talking to. These were the regulars. They were here every night, and probably drunk. I had to be a bit more specific. "Let me rephrase that. How many of you saw the piano player in here just a few moments ago?"

The hands disappeared.

"No one saw the piano player," I asked in amazement, "or heard the music?"

Nothing but blank expressions met my final question. I ran my hand over my face and took a long, deep breath. I needed sleep. I was obviously seeing things now. I walked carefully toward the exit. My head was swimming with doubt, confusion, and a heady dose of fear.

As I stepped out into the lobby I felt a meaty paw grab my arm and yank me toward the wall. I ripped my arm free and spun to find the Hispanic woman standing before me. "What the hell do you think you're doing?"

Her eyes were wide and she looked slightly panicked.

My anger instantly abated when I saw the fear in her expression. I started to reach for her to provide a bit of physical comfort, but she recoiled. I quickly held up my hands and patted the air. "It's okay. It's okay. You just startled me. That's all."

"The piano player," she whispered in perfect English. I'm not sure why, maybe I'm a racist, but I had expected choppy, broken English with a heavy Spanish accent. "I saw him too."

Her revelation was like a ray of light. "Really? Did you hear the music too?"

She nodded.

I shook my head. "Why didn't you raise your hand when I asked the question in there?"

"You're loco." She frowned. "I don't want to be associated with that."

I wasn't really sure what was unfolding here. She was creating more questions than answering. "Then why did you grab my arm out here to tell me you had seen the piano player?"

She pulled in a breath through her nose. "Because I saw him too."

"That's great." I came to the inescapable conclusion she was drunk, or one of those annoyingly needy people who will tell you anything so you pay attention to them for a moment. "You have a good night, ma'am." I turned away.

Her meaty paw ensured I wasn't going anywhere. She pulled me close and looked directly into my eyes. "I saw the piano player," she reiterated, "but he wasn't really there."

Yep. She was drunk.

I could smell the alcohol on her breath and this was no longer fun. "Listen, lady," I tried to hold my anger in, "you need to let go. I've had just about all I can take."

"You saw un espectro." The woman gasped as she looked into my eyes. "You can only stare into

46

the void for so long before it stares back into you." Finally letting go of my arm, she took an uneasy step back. Making the sign of the cross over her forehead and chest, she swung around and charged away.

I sighed in exhaustion.

Glancing down at my feet I spotted what looked like a business card on the floor. Glossy, black, and rectangular, I could see silver embossed lettering on its face but couldn't quite read it. Not fully understanding what compelled me to bend down and retrieve it, I held it in my hand for a long moment. Glancing over the text I felt a knot well up in my stomach as I read the card.

Angel Arroyo—Paranormal Investigator

I stood for a long moment in the hallway, the hairs on the back of my neck fully erect. What did she mean when she spoke about staring into the void? And what the hell was un espectro? Suddenly wishing I had paid more attention to Senior Santiago in high school Spanish, I looked out into the lobby but there was no trace of her. I slipped the card into my pocket slowly, hoping it wouldn't bite me.

I wondered if there was a memo I had missed somewhere regarding Scare Jack Devlin Day. After that quirky Devlinism, I think I needed to go back to bed. Today was just getting weirder by the moment and I hoped a new day would provide some relief.

Chapter Six

I couldn't have been more wrong.

"I'm sorry, Jack." James Baxter sighed and plopped my manuscript on his desk unceremoniously. "I don't see this as a best seller."

I had learned to really hate James during the course of our five year relationship. My editor was the first person to lay hands on my new manuscripts and had of late become the most cynical of them. An overly slender man, he never looked good in a suit even if it was perfectly tailored to him. It always seemed as if his bony frame didn't have enough mass to fill them out properly. With a beaklike nose and beady, brown eyes he looked more like a vulture ready to swoop down and peck out my organs. He was a good editor, of that there was no doubt, but I think his head had gotten too big for his office.

When I first defected to this publishing house, he was fresh out of college and thankful for the opportunity to work with an established name. I hate to sound egotistical—despite the fact I'm really good at it—but I am responsible for James' career. Now he was looking down on me. Isn't it funny how the worm turns? I wanted to get up and wrap my hands around his skinny chicken neck, but I remained composed. I nodded once to appear to take his criticism thoughtfully. "What do you see as the manuscript's biggest problem?"

James threw up his arms in disgust. "Where do I start?"

The tie knotted around my own throat was starting to feel a bit too tight. I was going to have to kill him. I understood that now. It's not that I can't take criticism—actually I don't handle it well—it's just that James is a little bitch. I hate to resort to name calling, but that's the best way to sum him up. He's a little bitch.

"Your characterization is weak," he answered. "I didn't care about any of the characters. They seemed like perverse caricatures hastily splattered on the page. It really seemed like you just wanted to kill people in this novel, and you just kept inventing boring characters to toss to their deaths. It's lazy writing." James shook his head. "And it's a vampire novel? That idea has been done to death. The market is glutted with terrible vampire novels right now."

Glancing down at my lap I saw my knuckles turning bright white, I was squeezing the arms of my chair so tightly. I expected them to snap at any moment. At least then I could take the fragments and beat James to death. "Okay," I breathed, "what would you suggest?"

"We need to tear the story down to plot and try again," James said without hesitation. A sly smirk grew over his thin lips, although it was barely visible beneath the shadow of the ski slope he called a nose. He was on a power trip, and he loved it.

"Back to plot?" I echoed angrily. "You want me to scrap the entire book?"

James nodded, smug in his position.

I shook my head. "What about Stephen King? Wasn't his last book about a spooky haunted lamp or something?"

James' expression remained unchanged.

My attempt at humor was lost. Maybe he thought I was serious. "The vampire is a great antagonist," I argued. "Renaldo," I said, referring to the character in my book as if he were real, "is almost the perfect killer."

"Almost," James acknowledged. "Except that he's pedestrian at best." My editor looked at my manuscript with disdain. "You never answer the most important question. This guy just shows up and kills people for no reason. Why is Renaldo there?"

"I thought the story was really simple," I answered. "He kills because he can, and he enjoys it." I paused and reconsidered my tactics. "I wanted to take the vampire back to being a terrible, soulless monster. Perhaps I overestimated my audience." It was a clear shot at James. I hope he caught it.

James sighed. "Well I didn't catch that."

Nope…swing and a miss.

"The book just isn't good, Jack." James adjusted himself in his chair. "I'm not trying to beat you down. It's just that readers expect a certain level of quality from a Jack Devlin novel. This," he said, motioning toward the manuscript as if it were a steaming pile of something, "just isn't it."

I leaned slowly forward in my chair. The venom that had been building during the meeting was reaching critical levels. I had taken enough and James was about to understand that. I had become Vesuvius, and this was the end of all things. Pulling a breath in through my nose, I held it in my lungs ready to unleash the torrent of angry expletives that I had been saving for a special occasion.

Then his phone beeped.

Lifting a single finger—the international symbol for *Give me a minute, I have to take this phone call that is obviously far more important than anything you could ever say*—James leaned forward in his magnificent, padded leather chair and tapped the phone on his glass desk with his free hand. "Go."

Good God! He can't even say hello? Where was the geeky, intelligent kid who wanted to be a writer and spoke passionately about the mythological themes in Star Wars? He was obviously dead and this was some sort of sick, twisted pod person bent on world domination. At any moment I expected him to cackle maniacally and threaten to launch nuclear missiles at the White House unless he was named Supreme Emperor of the World...but that may have been giving him too much credit.

"Mr. Baxter?" asked the voice of his secretary through the tinny speaker. "The CEO wants to see you."

I listened to Janice's soft and direct tone.

"Tell him I'm in a meeting that could last hours," James replied without taking his eyes off me.

I felt my skin crawl.

"I'm sorry, Mr. Baxter," Janice said unemotionally, "but he insisted. He wants to ask you something about your expense account."

I watched the color drain from James' face. His

gaze fell to the floor, certainly looking for an appropriate patch of carpet on which to vomit. I have to admit, I enjoyed watching his discomfort.

"Tell him," James stuttered, "that I will be there momentarily."

"Yes, Mr. Baxter," Janice replied before she severed the connection.

"Thank you, Janice," James said more to his shoes than the phone.

Letting his hand fall off the phone, he swiveled slowly in his chair and looked out of his tenth floor window at the magnificent cityscape stretching before him. I wondered if in that moment he was trying to find peace, or contemplating jumping through the glass.

There was a well-known rumor circulating through the building about James and his all-expense paid trip to the Caribbean earlier this year. Most claimed he had the company foot the bill by calling it a business trip. How he had slipped it under the radar was unknown, but it looked as if past sins were about to catch up with him. I would probably need a new editor. That didn't bother me as much as you might think.

He slowly turned back, his composure collected. It was a bluff. His poker face was getting better all the time. "I'm sorry, Jack," he said without even the slightest quiver in his voice, "seems we're going to have to reschedule." He stood up from his throne and adjusted his suit. "Please make arrangements with Janice, and I'll be in touch."

Walking around the desk, James extended his

52

hand to me. Looking down at his expectant palm, I thought for a moment about shaking it, but allowed the urge to pass. Instead, I turned my attention to James but made no movements. His face grew long and he slowly let the gesture of friendship fall away. I spoke more of my distaste for him in that moment than any diatribe I could have unleashed, and I'm pretty sure he received the message loud and clear. Stuffing the dejected hand into his pocket, he hung his head slightly and headed for the door. I heard Janice try and say something to James, but he rudely cut her off. With a grumble, James disappeared into the hallway that connected his office to the main lobby.

Standing, I looked around James' plush office. Bordered on two sides by floor-to-ceiling windows, it had a spectacular view of New York. Beyond the tan carpet, the concrete and glass skyscrapers seemed to march endlessly toward the ocean. And on a clear day, a person could actually see the curvature of the planet. It was breathtaking. I've often wondered what it would be like to have an office like this with an entire city at my feet. But my vocation took me to other vistas, other places. This wasn't where I belonged. This was James' dream, not mine.

Turning away, I loosened my black tie and undid the top button on my shirt. I let out a long, slow breath and started to relax. I wasn't going to waste any more time on James today. Spinning slowly, my eyes fell on my novel. Stacked on the editor's desk exactly where he had dropped it, the novel seemed somehow sad and rejected. Snatching my manuscript, I tucked it under my arm and moved toward the door.

I stopped short and found myself staring at Janice.

I guess I really hadn't been paying attention to her before the meeting because of my displeasure in being there, but she looked stunning today. Swathed in a form-fitting black business jacket, her white blouse was unbuttoned just enough so I could see her lacy pink bra peeking out. With blond hair spilling around her perfect face the same color as exotic beaches I had only glimpsed in magazines, she easily outclassed the view in James' office. I watched her work on her computer for a moment then become aware of my presence. Looking up quizzically, her expression quickly softened when she realized I was staring. She laughed sweetly.

Trying to move as confidently as I could, I played as if my chin itched when really I was checking for drool. "Hey, Janice."

"Mr. Devlin," she greeted me.

"Jack," I corrected.

She cocked her head slightly.

"Jack," I repeated. "How many times have I asked you to call me Jack?"

"That would be inappropriate," Janice retorted mechanically. "Mr. Baxter has made it very clear I am to address all of his clients formally."

I started to argue, but let it die. It wouldn't do any good anyway.

Folding her hands on her desk, she looked patiently at me.

I couldn't think of anything to say. Me: A

54

professional writer and tongue-tied. I had to say something as the silence became deafening. All I could come up with was, "So, catch any of the Giant's games?" Smooth, Devlin…real smooth.

"I don't like football," Janice replied.

"Me neither," I answered.

She couldn't hide the mixture of amusement and confusion on her face. "Then why did you ask?"

I thought about it for a moment then finally shrugged. "I have no idea. Just trying to make small talk."

Janice laughed again. It was soft and unpretentious, but fragile enough that I felt it could break at any moment. She always seemed so alive, even when life was intent on breaking her. "You don't get out much, do you? Oh, wait," she exclaimed as if someone bit her. "I almost forgot!"

I stared at her vacantly as she quickly rummaged over the paperwork on her desk. Lifting up a short stack of folders, she snatched a small, yellow note and handed it to me.

"Your agent called while you were in the meeting," she explained. "She said she was able to pull some strings and get you in."

"In?" I asked curiously, "Into what?" Lifting the note, I saw my fate scribbled in thick, black ink:

11:00 AM Tomorrow—HorrorCon, Booth #1104

My heart sank. My agent had been toying with the idea of having me at this damned convention, but I didn't think she would actually do it. It had seemed more like an idle threat than anything else.

She kept saying to me, "David, if you don't get this book done on schedule, I'm going to book you at the New York HorrorCon." I had hoped she was just joking.

"You'll love it," Janice replied exuberantly. "My boyfriend and I go every year. We even dress up as our favorite horror characters. Last year I was Elvira."

"HorrorCon." I sighed. Why did life feel the need to kick the crap out of me today? Although the thought of Janice in a black wig, tight black dress, and showing her voluptuous cleavage did lessen the pain a bit. "Are you and your boyfriend going to be there this year?"

"Of course," she answered with an excited wiggle. A shadow passed over her face as she beckoned me close to her. Leaning down over her desk, she spoke in a hushed tone. "Did you see the movie X-Men?"

I nodded.

"I'm going to dress up as Mystique this year," Janice admitted quietly.

"But she was practically naked," I blurted before realizing I had even said it.

She nodded. Janice leaned back in her chair, her blue eyes sparkling deviously. "I've been working on the costume for months," she admitted. "I had to take a plaster mold of my entire body."

I slowly straightened my spine. "That will be," I thought of Janice with blue skin, red hair, and nearly naked, "interesting."

"I promise to come visit your booth, Mr. Devlin," Janice added. All of the mischievousness I had just witnessed was completely gone. She was back to her usual, perky, normal self.

"Thank you, Janice," I said, turning away, "I'm looking forward to it." And that was my exit cue. Turning, I headed toward the elevator on the far side of the lobby. I hung my head. It was probably best not to tempt fate any further. It already seemed like it had it in for me.

Digging my cell from my pocket, I cycled through several contacts hastily added before I left the hotel this morning. Hitting the send button, I pressed the phone to my ear and checked my watch hoping it wasn't too late. As the fourth ring sounded in my ear, I heard a click and a woman's voice answer. "Cynthia?" I paused and listened to her response. "It's Jack Devlin." Tapping the elevator call button, I shot one more fleeting glance over my shoulder at Janice, as if hoping she would stop me. Unfortunately, her focus had already shifted back to her work.

I felt my grip tighten on the phone. "I want to see The Hollow again. Yeah, tomorrow afternoon," I confirmed. "Go ahead and start drawing up the paperwork. Thanks, Cynthia."

Two soft chimes signaled the lift's arrival. Letting the phone fall from my ear, I thumbed the end button and stuffed it back in my pocket. The elevator's doors slid open. With a half-hearted sigh, I adjusted the manuscript under my arm, stepped in, and pressed the lobby button.

Chapter Seven

Unlike big brother New York, the sleepy suburb of Union rolled up the sidewalks at ten. Shops closed down, traffic lessened, and residents scurried home on slick streets trying to evade the bitter cold. Heavy gray skies that had been threatening precipitation all day finally fulfilled their warning and released their frozen cargo. Snowflakes tumbled gently toward the ground in an archaic ballet, creating an almost surreal peacefulness that blanketed the town. Watching out the window of the cab, I spotted what, to me, looked like an oasis. Tapping the cab's divider, I altered my destination.

Warm, yellow light of the town's only twenty-four hour coffee shop spilled out onto the sidewalk around me. I stood transfixed, as if gazing upon the very face of God. My novel still tucked safely under my arm, I pushed through the door and stepped inside. The rich fragrance of coffee and pastries immediately wrapped around and soothed me as no other smell in the world could. My eyes wandered over a few warmly-dressed patrons sipping their steaming beverages and enjoying lively conversations. Taking in a heady whiff of the atmosphere, I brushed the snow from my shoulders, smiled, and stepped up to the front counter.

I had come home.

A cute blond barista emerged from the back, spotted me, and quickly made her way toward the register. She couldn't have been more than twenty, and the tight curves of her body confirmed that. A raven-black baby doll t-shirt didn't leave much to the imagination, but the maroon apron she wore over the top helped. Adjusting her stylish, black-rimmed glasses, she locked eyes with me and smiled. "What can I get for you?"

"Venti vanilla latte please," I answered, not needing to look at the menu hanging above the counter.

Grabbing a thick, brown cup from a nearby stack, she noted the order on it with a Sharpie and set it aside. Running her fingertips over the register, it whirred and clicked as it processed. Telling me the total, she waited.

Digging my debit card from my wallet, I handed it over. "Busy tonight?"

She slid my card through the built-in reader and handed it back. "Not too bad. I think the snow's keeping people at home."

I nodded. "I would have thought the snow would make people want something warm to drink."

"Makes sense to me," she said, handing me the receipt. "Give me just a minute to make your drink."

"Thanks," I said with a smile.

Snatching my cup from the counter, she turned and started to prepare my order. The familiar hiss of the machines sounded as she quickly went to work.

"You work here long?"

She looked back at me as she filled the cup. "About three months. It's just part-time while I'm in college."

"Ah," I replied. "What's your major?"

"English," the blond barista answered as she moved from machine to machine.

"Teacher?" I asked.

"Writer," she corrected.

"That's very cool," I smiled. "You mean like technical writer, or something?"

The barista smiled, almost as if embarrassed. "Novelist. I love to write literary fiction."

It's amazing what you can find if you just look. "Genre?"

"Horror," the barista replied.

I realized there was a strong possibility I was facing my future competition. At least she was cute. "Good for you," I said with an evil smile. "It's a tough industry to break into, but if you persevere and practice, you can make it."

Noticing my grin and the manuscript tucked under my arm for the first time, she put two and two together. "You're a writer? Published writer…?"

"Yeah," I breathed. I reached my hand toward her. "Jack Devlin, horror novelist."

She laughed. "I've read one of your books." The barista snapped the lid on my cup. "I actually wanted to come see you tomorrow at HorrorCon, but I couldn't get time off." Setting the beverage before me, she placed her hands nervously on the edge of the counter, obviously working up the courage to ask a question.

There are generally three questions published authors receive from upcoming novelists: 1) How did you become a published author? 2) Can you read my stuff? 3) Can you submit my manuscript to your agent/publisher? As much as I like encouraging the next generation of writers, I hate answering these questions. I really feel becoming a published author is more about the journey than anything else. There are hundreds of books published every year on how to publish books. It seems like cheating, or reading the last page of a mystery novel. And of course, there was always the "Why are you published (you no-talent hack) when I'm not?" factor to deal with. I just hated that. Maybe it's just me though. As I looked at the face of my young, blond barista, I knew she was leaning heavily toward question two, but three was still a possibility.

"Can I ask you a question?" she asked.

"You just did," I replied, hopefully flustering her a bit.

She shook it off, undeterred, "I'm sure you must get this all the time, but…"

Here it comes.

"…what do you think is the most important thing to develop my writing?"

I cocked an eyebrow and paused. That wasn't what she was supposed to ask. She wasn't looking for the easy road. She really wanted advice. I faltered, unsure what to say. "I suppose," I took a breath and grabbed my coffee, "the most important thing is to read everything you can get your hands on, and keep writing."

She nodded, understanding. "That's what I've been doing. Just wanted to make sure I was on the right path."

"Seems that way," I answered.

"Well," the young woman smiled broadly, apparently happy with my response, "I won't take up any more of your time, Mr. Devlin. Thank you, and enjoy your coffee."

I took a sip of my latte. The hot beverage seared my tongue, but I didn't want to look like a hopping idiot in front of this obviously intelligent young woman. "You're welcome." I started to turn from the counter but paused. "I'm sorry, I didn't even ask your name."

"Roxanne Crisp," she answered.

"It's nice to meet you, Roxanne," I said with the overwhelming urge to bust out singing The Police classic. "I'll keep an eye out for your name on the best seller's lists," I said with a smile.

Roxanne laughed. "You better."

Was that a threat? I laughed out loud. She had just officially become my favorite person on this trip. "I think I'm going to be moving here to Union," I added completely out of character. "I hope we run into each other again."

"Me too," the young novelist agreed sweetly.

Turning away, I spotted a quiet table in the corner. Weaving through the maze of seating arrangements, I set my novel and beverage on the light wood table. Sliding into the chair, I peered at the snow falling outside the large windows and could feel the cold radiating inside. The flakes were steadily growing in size and density. It looked like Union could have a full-blown blizzard on its hands. Looking back to the table, I ran my fingertips over my novel's title page. Not to personify it too much, but it seemed sad, and yet somehow relieved to be back in my hands. I had no idea my meeting with James would turn into a rescue mission. Of course, I was only delaying the inevitable. He already had a contract for this novel. I just wanted to make him sweat for a while.

"Hiya, Jack."

As I looked up and my eyes locked with hers, I felt a shiver run down my back. You know those stop-motion animation movies by the impressively warped Tim Burton? Yeah. I swear one of the marionettes had stepped out of the film and, in all of her gothic glory hovered before me. Her head, looking almost too bulbous for her slender neck, had huge icy blue eyes and a tiny mouth painted with black lip gloss that seemed horrifically disproportionate. Her greasy black hair fell down around her face, almost hiding it. Strands of royal purple were woven in, and highlighted a messy ponytail pulled onto the top of her head that seemed to sprout like a fountain in all directions. Her slender, almost anorexic frame was swathed in black from her neck down to the huge combat boots she wore on her feet. But her most striking feature was her skin. She was chalk white, devoid of any of the color of living flesh. Bluish veins were visible beneath the surface while her eyes slowly sank into graying pits. She looked as if she had been dead for some time.

"Hello, Wednesday." I had no idea what her real name was, but that seemed to sum her up pretty accurately.

"Wednesday." The evil marionette rolled the nickname over her palette, sampling it. Sitting in the chair opposite mine at the small table, she shifted and crossed her legs seductively. She stared at me, unblinking, with her unnatural frosty blue eyes. "I'm sorry, Jack, I like the name, but I don't get the reference."

"Wednesday," I said again. "You know, the spooky daughter from the Addams Family show? The one who cut the heads off her dolls?"

Wednesday shrugged and pulled a lock of purple hair away from her face with her pinky. "I thought that was Pugsley?"

"Doesn't really matter," I added. The black leather trench coat wrapped around her slender frame was completely dry, showing no trace of the heavy falling snow outside. "If you don't mind, I'd like to be alone. I'm leaving now."

"You won't make it two steps," Wednesday promised.

It wasn't an idle threat. She was dangerous. That much I was certain of. Straightening my back, I lifted my drink and took a sip. Letting the hot coffee slide down my throat, I tried to concoct some sort of battle plan as anger started to build in my chest. "What do you want?"

"For a writer, you're a bit dim," she said with an almost playful quality about her voice. "You're asking the wrong questions, Jack."

I wanted to lash out, to jump across the table and smash Wednesday's head into the tabletop, but wasn't sure that was the best course of action in a public place, or any place for that matter. My fingers slid around the edge of the table and squeezed.

The evil puppet tilted her head slightly so her eyebrows seductively shadowed her large eyes. "You can't go stumbling blindly and expect to trip over the truth. Hunting for EVPs, or crawling through dusty old houses with your flashlight isn't the way to find Irene," Wednesday scolded.

The sound of my wife's name sliding off her tongue only enraged me further.

"You sit there and talk as if you know me, as if we've been friends for years." I looked up and down Wednesday trying to discern some hint of who, or, for that matter, what she really was. "You don't know me. You don't have the right."

"I know more than you think." Wednesday sneered.

"You know," I shot up from my seat, "I understand why you gothic kids have such a high suicide rate now. If I had to sit here and listen to you all day, I'd kill myself too!" I snatched my novel and coffee from the table. "Luckily, for us both, I don't have to."

"I warned you," Wednesday hissed, but held her position.

I froze...but that little voice clawed harder at the back of my head. I wanted to bolt, but couldn't seem to convince my feet to cooperate. Stuck in place, I stared the evil, living doll down.

Wednesday scowled.

The sound of glass shattering ripped my attention away from Wednesday. As my heart jumped, my eyes diverted to the main counter. Roxanne stood with a shocked expression, her hands still holding the imaginary coffee mug she had just dropped. Refocusing, I turned back to Wednesday—

She was gone.

I felt my heart flitter in my ribcage. Knowing for certain I hadn't taken my attention off her for more than four seconds, I couldn't fathom how she had simply disappeared. I would have seen her move out of the corner of my eye. My eyes settled on the chair she had been perched in. No trace of the creepy, gothic woman remained, not even a telltale puddle on the floor from the melting snow on her shoes. She had simply vanished.

I looked back up to where Roxanne had just been standing. "Did you just see a girl with black hair in here?"

Roxanne peeked over the counter as she swept up the broken porcelain. "What?"

"Girl," I repeated almost frantically, pointing to the chair where Wednesday had been seated. "Creepy. Black hair. Did you see her?"

Roxanne shrugged. "No, sorry."

I sighed as a snide remark leapt onto my tongue, but I let it slide. Roxanne had just been doing her job, and didn't deserve to be the brunt of my abuse.

Turning away from the counter, I stared out into the heavily falling snow. The once peaceful feeling had been completely shattered by Wednesday's appearance. She had gone beyond simple nut job, and with her verbal threat, had turned dangerous. Honestly, I wasn't sure what to do. To involve local law enforcement at this point would just make a mess. For the time being, anyway, I would handle this myself.

Glancing down at my watch, I walked quickly out of the coffee shop and into the snow. I had to get some rest. Tomorrow was going to be a very busy day. I was attending HorrorCon, plus there were calls to make, funds to transfer, and papers to sign. I was buying a house.

Chapter Eight

HorrorCon was littered with monsters, aliens, and goblins of all shapes and sizes. Costumes ranged from magnificent to ludicrous and everything in between. They wove in and around the sometimes grand, other times modest booths on their quest for horror related memorabilia. As I stepped fully into the massive room, a neon green Tyrannosaurus rex crashed passed me with its stubby arms full of Night of the Living Dead merchandise.

The only thought that entered my twisted brain was, Why isn't he dressed as a zombie? Maybe he was a zombie dinosaur? Yeah. That was just stupid.

As awe hit me, I think I had to physically close my agape mouth. Dropping my head and hoping not to be recognized, I kept my gaze firmly on the maroon paisley carpet. With only a casual upward glance to check the prominently displayed booth numbers, I slowed as I neared the eleven hundreds. Spotting my booth, I let out a long sigh. Smooshed between a Xena, Warrior Princess collectibles booth, and another that was constantly blaring a looped copy of Michael Jackson's Thriller—complete with fog machines and two scantily-clad, dancing, zombie booth bunnies—mine was a little on the pitiful side. It seemed that everyone else in the convention had gone all out, but my agent had deemed a simple banner and a table would be enough. As I scanned over the red lettering on the boring white background, I stopped and ran my hand down my face. That was just great. Really great.

My name was spelled wrong.

I'm sure everyone is going to be clamoring for an autographed novel by Jack Devin. What? Never heard of him? That makes two of us.

Sliding around the wobbly, plastic table I spotted a few, scant boxes of books, a couple of outdated glossy photos (I recognized the long since shaved 90's style goatee), and a box of cheap pens with my latest novel's title on it. Wow, my agent had gone all out on this one. I was going to have to thank her…assuming I ever saw her again. It was starting to seem more and more like I was getting boned. I figured by the end of the day I wasn't going to have an agent. I'm certain my publishing contract was next as fate seemed dead set on kicking me square in the junk.

Or maybe I was just being gloomy.

Dropping down into the metal folding chair—which was bent and sloped forward, by the way—I reached down and popped my first box of books open. Snatching a few of the hardcovers out, I set them up in a little display on the front of my table. It would in no way compete with the hot zombies next door, but it was something. You know that part in Thriller that Vincent Price does the voice over and then drops his maniacal, mad scientist laugh? Having already heard it twice since arriving, it started to grate on my nerves. I think Mr. Price was going to have an accident before the end of the day. I would have to see to that.

I glanced down at my watch. It wasn't quite

eleven. Sighing, I dropped my head into my hands. To make matters worse, I was early. The day kept getting better and better.

"Mr. Devlin? Or should I say Mr. Devin?"

Looking up, I found the source of the familiar voice but wasn't sure how to reply.

First, it was a stupid joke, and second, she was completely blue. Forcing myself to remain focused on her face, I tried to ignore her half-naked, blue body. Her shoulder-length hair was dyed fire-red and an intense pair of yellow contacts completely transformed her eyes into horrible demon orbs. I wasn't entirely sure how she had done it, but a thin layer of latex covered her breasts and groin making her resemble a proto human. Rows of tiny spikes, almost reptilian in design, ran over her shoulders, fingertips, and down her legs. Her curves, pronounced by the blue body paint and lack of clothing covering them, looked incredible. Much like the mutant's ability she was emulating, she had completely transformed into Mystique.

"You look fantastic, Janice," I breathed, fighting the urge to jump the table and pounce on her.

As my editor's personal assistant, I had become well acquainted with Janice. She had spoken to me on the phone more times than my editor had, and was always a bright spot during my visits to New York. A sweet, young twenty-something who didn't care for fame or anyone connected with it, Janice was a secretary and that was it. Her sense of identity was remarkable for someone her age. She knew exactly what she wanted, and what it was going to take to get it. Yet, there was nothing questionable or nefarious about her ways. She just wanted to be happy. Truly, Janice was one of the wisest people I had ever known. I often thought about dropping to my knees before her and saying, Teach me. I'm sure she would just laugh softly and pat me mockingly on the head.

My eyes fell on her boyfriend. Dressed from head to toe in black, some sort of pseudo cape with red satin lining hung from his neck. The most laughable feature of his costume was the domed bucket planted firmly on his head. Glistening red with purple highlights around the T-shaped visor, he looked more like a dildo than the super villain he pretended to be. I couldn't actually make out much of the man though, as the costume did a good job of hiding his features. All I could see were his piercing blue eyes.

"Mr. Devlin," Janice slipped an arm around her boyfriend in a very intimate gesture, "this is Grace."

"Grace," I mouthed the oddly feminine name. Although a bit taller than me—I wasn't entirely sure if it was natural or because of the phallic helmet on his head—I was certain I could take him.

"Nice to meet you, Mr. Devlin," Grace said in a deep, dark voice that seemed to come from some unnatural blood pact with a demon rather than his mouth. "I'm a big fan of your work."

"Thank you." I eyed the young man warily as I slid back into my uncomfortably slanted chair. I generally didn't accept compliments from people I didn't know as they struck me as hollow—the compliments, not the people. It was time to test his knowledge. "What's your favorite novel of mine?"

"Five 'Til Midnight," Grace replied.

That was considered by most, including me, to be my best novel. I wondered if he actual knew what he was talking about. "Why did you like it?"

"Rowe's characterization," Grace replied matter-of-factly, as if he actually knew what he was talking about. "The idea of a soldier torn between protecting his country and assassinating the commander-in-chief was extremely well played out. I mean," he started to gesture with his hands emphatically, "to go from one extreme as a sworn protector to a killer was amazingly well designed."

Well, at least he was right. "Thanks, Grace." Creating both the hero and the villain of the piece in the same character was something I'd always wanted to try. Dammit, I was starting to like this kid.

Janice tightened her grip on the man.

"What I find most interesting though is how Rowe's story mirrored Dante's decent into Hell," Grace added.

Having heard the comparison before, it was familiar, but I certainly hadn't intentionally put it in the novel. And I would never compare my work to the genius that was Dante Alighieri.

"Rowe falls deeper and deeper into darkness," Grace continued, "and each of the major moments in his life is like Dante reaching another level of Hell. Like when Rowe first discovers the parallels between the war and the President's plot, he descends to the first level."

That actually made sense. He had read the

book, and more importantly, taken away a deeper appreciation of the text than even I had intended. I extended my hand in a gesture of respect. "It's very nice to meet you, Grace," I said sincerely.

Janice grinned at my acceptance of her beau.

An attention chime interrupted our conversation.

As a hush fell over the crowd, a barely distinguishable announcer warbled a message over the convention hall's public address system that sounded more like a swarm of angry bees than anything resembling English. Managing to pick out a few words and phrases that sounded almost human, I gathered that the costume contest was about to begin in the main auditorium.

As the costumed masses started their exodus toward the promise of prizes and fifteen minutes of fame and glory, I was, of course, thankful they were leaving.

"It was nice seeing you, Mr. Devlin," Janice said and started to maneuver Grace toward the auditorium.

"Wait," I dug into the box of books below my lame, plastic table and retrieved a copy of Five 'Til Midnight, "let me autograph a book for Grace."

"We really need to get in there to register," Janice said apologetically.

"Hold on," Grace countered. "I want his autograph. It'll only take a minute."

Janice shot her boyfriend a quick glance of annoyance, but acquiesced.

I smiled at Grace despite myself. Dropping the book on the desk, I flipped open the cover and hastily scrawled my name on the title page. I couldn't help it. I was really starting to like him. I slid the book toward its recipient. "Thanks, Grace. Good luck in the contest."

Snatching it up, Grace held it as if it were a rare treasure. "Thanks, Mr. Devlin."

With that, the two turned and headed toward the auditorium. Sliding in with a few stragglers, they disappeared inside. My hair stood on end as Vincent Price cackled again. I had the overwhelming urge to tear into the next booth swinging, but somehow, someway, found the patience to withstand it. I dropped my head onto the table with a thud. Only eleven thirty, I knew it would be a long goddamned day.

"I hate that fucking song."

"Amen," I replied, face still flat on the desk.

Lifting my head, revulsion hit me squarely in the chest and almost knocked the wind out of my lungs.

"Jack." Wednesday spoke my name with an almost unearthly satisfaction.

She watched me with an utter stillness that sent shivers down to my toes.

"You're about to miss the start of the costume contest," I offered, hoping to get rid of her.

She cocked her head, looking like a dog trying to comprehend astrophysics. "Costume?"

"I just assumed," I said, gesturing to her outfit but let the thought fade before I dug an even bigger hole. Swallowing hard, I nodded. "What do you want, Wednesday?"

"You always ask the wrong question," the

74

living marionette rebuked with a scolding wave of her finger.

"What's the right question?" I asked, obviously confused.

Her wicked smile grew into a sinister sneer. "It's what I can do for you," she answered enigmatically.

Now I really wanted to run and hide. "Pardon?"

Leaning forward, she bent at the hips—I don't know any other way to describe it other than "unnaturally"—and placed her palms flat on my crappy table. "I know what you want," the evil marionette teased in a hushed, playful tone.

I sat straight up as if a blade were jammed into my back. "If you're thinking you have anything that I want, Wednesday," I said, pointing to the cadaver's body before me, "you are sorely mistaken."

"You're a fucking pig," she snarled and her face contorted with anger. Just as quickly as the rage appeared, it vanished and was replaced with dead calm. "But I already knew that."

She already knew that? Who was this freak of nature? And where was security when I needed them?

"You are searching for the truth," the marionette said as if she were casually talking about the weather. "Searching for your dead wife."

The imaginary knife blade jammed deeper into my back and twisted.

I felt the urge to get away from her—anyway I could—as my skin started to crawl. "How do you know...?" I cursed myself as the last consonant left my lips. Unintentionally, I had verified her statement and given her an entrance into my personal life. It was stalker psychology 101. I, of course, was an idiot.

Wednesday's smile was as wide as the cat's that had just eaten the canary, and easily as satisfied. She shifted her weight from foot to foot ever so slightly. "I am the truth you seek."

Horrified, I shot up and pushed myself into the doll's face without thought of reprimand. The metal folding chair clattered angrily to the floor causing anyone who wasn't already watching the exchange to turn and stare. "I have had just about enough of this cryptic Yoda bullshit," I growled. "I don't know who you are, or what you want, but I'm not playing anymore."

"Jack," the evil marionette cooed, "I really think you should calm down." She slowly straightened up and looked derisively at me. "If you ever want to see Irene again."

My dead wife's name felt like a solid gut punch.

The urge to lash out and strike her was becoming too overwhelming. She was toying with me. I gripped the table angrily to keep my hands in place. "Leave."

Starting to protest, Wednesday raised her eyebrow curiously. "I don't think—"

"Leave!" I barked and slammed my fist down completely cutting off her retort.

She didn't react to my threat.

But I held my ground.

"Fine," Wednesday hissed. Sighing, she finally

took a step back. "I guess you don't know what the fuck you want." Her eyes looked coal black in her rage. Spinning, she turned and started away from me. "Have fun with Ezekiel," she shot over her shoulder as she rounded a stretch of booths and vanished.

Gritting my teeth, I felt a wave of fear and anger hit me like a tidal wave. I thought for a moment about chasing the evil marionette down, but I wisely let the thought die. Looking down at my hands, I slowly unclenched them to reveal deep red nail marks in my palms. As I straightened up, I took a breath and tried to swallow my rage. It burned like battery acid and threatened to backwash into my mouth at any moment.

Then I must've finally processed her parting words as they hit me like a brick. Have fun with the Ezekiel? Remembering my encounter in The Hollow, I watched the goose bumps rise on my flesh. What the hell was wrong with that girl? I was certain it wasn't anything a little Prozac couldn't clear up, but the question remained: How did she know so much about me?

I wasn't sure how to deal with that.

After lifting my hand, I rubbed the bridge of my nose. I closed my eyes and exhaled. I think I had endured just about enough of this place. I eyed the convention hall exit with one thought in mind: I needed a cigarette and a good, stiff drink.

Chapter Nine

As Cynthia and I stood in the foyer of The Hollow, the hairs on the back of my neck stood up. The same voice that shrieked at Wednesday clawed at the back of my skull as I remembered the black mass. It took everything I had to not grab Cynthia's hand and hold on for reassurance. Slipping my laptop back off my shoulder, I set it carefully against the wall. My eyes instinctively wandered to the top of the stairs as I stood back up. Warm light filtered through the large glass windows, creating a very peaceful scene. Even so, my instincts were in fight or flight mode, but there was no way I would run again. I wanted to be here.

She could be here.

Still drowning in her yellow realtor jacket, Cynthia had at least chosen to roll up the sleeves so it almost appeared to fit her. My paperwork, freshly signed, was slung protectively under her arm in a thick manila envelope. She seemed somehow relieved as she looked over the foyer, as if she knew she didn't have to come back here anymore. I wondered for a moment if there was some kind of bet down at her office about who would actually be able to sell The Hollow.

After all, who wanted to buy a haunted house?

"Here's the key to your new home, Jack," Cynthia said, handing me a jingling key ring. She beamed with excitement, probably from the fat commission check she had just earned. "A copy of the paperwork will be sent over tomorrow afternoon."

Snatching the key, I held it in my hand. Twisting it ever so slightly, I watched the light gleam off its polished, silver surface. There's something almost magical about a key. A gateway device, it opens portals to new places and new experiences that couldn't otherwise be obtained. Of course, no gateway comes without a price, and this was no exception. Once I slipped it into my pocket, it felt heavy as if it were weighing me down. I realized it was only my imagination, but that didn't make me feel any better.

I turned back to Cynthia and forced a smile. "Thank you for all of your help."

Cynthia returned the gesture. "My pleasure, Jack. You have my phone number?"

I nodded.

She took one final look around the house then pulled in a deep breath as if a weight had just been lifted. "Is there anything else I can do for you?"

"No," I exhaled. "I think I'm good."

Before the last consonant had rolled off my tongue, Cynthia was outside and pulling the front door shut. "Have a good night!"

Slam.

I stared at the door in awe. Then it hit me: she knew more than she was letting on. That much had just become obvious. But how much did she really know? I wondered if there were any local myths or legends surrounding the house or the death of Mr. Ezekiel. A devious grin spread across my lips. I would have to invite Cynthia back for a little housewarming dinner.

Turning back, I rested my hands on my hips and inspected my new purchase. It didn't bother me that I had no actual intent of living here. My home was in Southern Idaho, this, I shrugged…was more of a science project on an insane scale. The Hollow smelled old, like a museum. Dusty trinkets that possibly contained some mysterious value and moldy books overpowered the home's aroma. The atmosphere was dense and still, as if even it came to this place to die. But there was a lingering, subtle fragrance in the air I couldn't quite identify. It was an almost botanical bouquet with the distinct flavor of women's perfume. There was something familiar about it, yet alien at the same time. It was almost as if I knew this scent, but not how or from where. The memory was elusive, as if by design.

The scent dissipated leaving me strangely uncomfortable. A deep sense of loneliness and despair washed through me, but it wasn't internal. It felt as though the emotions were being forced upon me. Unsure if it was a trick of my brain or the emotions assaulting me, the foyer seemed to darken. As goose bumps rose across my flesh, I was overtaken by the urge to flee. Almost overwhelming, I fought against it and kept my feet planted in place.

Holding my hand against the wall for support, I knelt down next to my laptop bag and opened the front pocket. Slipping my hand in, I shifted through the junk accumulated there. Digging a rectangular, plastic object free, I righted it in my palm and thumbed the controls. Jet-black, smooth, and roughly the size of a pack of cigarettes, this was an

Electromagnetic Field detector. Commonly referred to as an 'EMF meter,' the device detected fluctuations in magnetic, electric and radio/microwave energy levels that were invisible to the naked eye. There was a commonly held, albeit controversial, theory that paranormal activity created anomalous readings that could be measured with this device. But then again, so did a toaster. Still, it was something.

Retrieving my lucky green flashlight from the laptop bag, I stood and started slowly across the foyer. Sweeping the EMF meter carefully before me, I tried to create a base reading to start from. The digital display cycled from zero point zero one to zero point two, but remained fairly constant. That wasn't considered a substantial reading by any means. Nearing the stairs, the LCD climbed quickly to two point six and I felt an uneasy quiver in my stomach. Swinging the meter away from the stairs, I watched the reading drop back down to baseline. Rotating back, the spike returned.

I lifted my foot and placed it gingerly on the stairs. The wood creaked and groaned. Summoning all of my courage, I stepped up. Glancing nervously at my EMF meter, the reading held steady at three point zero. My focus shifted to the landing above me and I couldn't help but think of the black mass. My legs felt heavy as I ascended the stairs. As if I were walking in thick mud, each step became harder to take. Nearing the landing, the EMF reading jumped to three point nine. There was something here. The warm morning light washed over me and provided some relief, but the lingering memory was hard to escape. Taking one final step, I stood exactly where I had seen it. I looked down at the shaking meter in my hand.

Nine point three.

Gulping down a breath, I scanned over the rectangular landing. The stairs split into two sections that wound up on the left and the right. A span of decorative railing stretched between the two stairwells on the second floor and offered an amazing view out of the large windows that reached all the way to the top of the cathedral ceiling. Two large ferns stood on either side of the window like silent sentries guarding this sacred space. It would have been quite peaceful if I didn't feel like running screaming from the house.

Scanning the meter slowly over the landing, I watched the display spike wildly from zero point two to eighteen point three.

I had only encountered readings like this one other time: the fabled Winchester Mystery House in California. Supposedly one of the most haunted places in the world, the house is a maze of dead ends and hallways that lead nowhere. Built by the heiress to the Winchester rifle fortune, most believe she went quite mad after the deaths of her husband and daughter. She claimed the spirits of those killed by Winchester weapons wanted her to continually build and remodel the house or they would kill her. Work continued every day for nearly forty years until her death. During one of the daily tours, I had packed my EMF along and found some interesting readings, but that was it. There was no sense of dread like I felt here. This was something different.

Circling around, I started toward the right staircase. Turning my back on the landing, I felt a tingle up my neck as though a cobweb had landed on my flesh and was slowly being pulled away. I wanted to look, but couldn't bring myself to turn around. Paralysis set in as my fear grew uncontrollably. My legs refused to work. Closing my eyes, I drew a deep breath in through my nose and summoned every remaining shred of strength I had left. The feeling intensified as I took that first step. I knew, in that moment, there was something behind me, reaching for me. Each step I took away from the landing quickened until I leapt over the last three stairs. Hitting the top, I spun, grabbed the railing, and stared back down at the landing.

I stood transfixed, like a man in a trance.

I could have sworn that Death himself had been standing behind me a moment ago, its bony fingers a breath away from my flesh, yet as I looked into the warm yellow sunlight spilling in through the dirty windowpanes, I found absolutely nothing. As my heart rate began to normalize, I lifted the EMF and stared at the screen. The reading cycled from zero point zero to zero point four, but nothing more. I let the meter fall to my side and gradually let my gaze drop from the landing.

What the hell was going on?

Dread hit me, slid down and settled like a rock in my stomach. The hairs on my arms stood up as the cobweb slid across the back of my neck again. I gritted my teeth. This time I was going to look. Gripping my metal flashlight like a weapon, I tensed my muscles and spun. I stared into the empty second floor hallway, my back to the stairs. Furrowing my brow, I lifted my EMF meter hoping to find some explanation. My eyes widened uncontrollably as I stared at the digital display. The screen was almost black as the numbers cycled too quickly to read.

"Oh shi—"

As if an invisible fist slammed into my sternum, the wind was knocked out of me. My heel slipped off the top step as the force of the blow propelled me back.

I fell.

My arms flailed wildly as I spilled backwards. I hit hard, the edge of the stair slamming into my lower back. Stars sparkled in front of my eyes as pain surged up and exploded into my brain. The world blurred as I tumbled. The back of my head cracked against the hard wood and I felt my arm fold angrily beneath me. Hitting the landing, my body throbbed in agony.

Lying in a heap, I groaned. Lifting myself off the floor, I propped the sack of potatoes I called my body up against the wall. I hurt, but I didn't think anything was broken. Gasping in pain as my back throbbed angrily, I quickly leaned on my elbow to reduce the pressure. Running my hand through my hair, I felt a quickly growing knot on the back of my head. That was a good sign. At least I didn't have a concussion.

I scanned the top of the staircase expecting to find the dark mass observing my pain mockingly, but found it as empty as before. Grabbing my chest and leaning over, I painfully sucked air back into my lungs. Spotting my EMF detector near one of the ferns, I pulled myself toward it and was finally able to grab it. After flipping it over in my hand, I sighed. The LCD had been smashed in the fall. Dark blobs of liquid crystals pooled beneath the cracked glass that splintered out like a spider's web.

Tossing the trashed EMF detector aside, I pulled my hand over my face. The muscles in my back ached. I was going to need a new meter, I sighed, and some Icy Hot. I took another pain-filled breath into my lungs and looked at the empty landing atop the stairs. This wasn't exactly how I imagined my first night in my new house.

Chapter Ten

Her blood was everywhere.

A trail stretched from the bathroom, across the tiled kitchen floor, and was now soaking into the beige living room carpet creating an ever-growing red stain. Holding her in my arms, her head slumped on my shoulder while her arms fell wide. I shook her limp, lifeless body hoping vainly to wake her.

I didn't know what to do.

Splattered angrily up her arms and chest, blood created an evil rainbow across her white t-shirt. The cuts on her wrists were so deep that I swore I could see muscles and tendons. And it wasn't the romantic image Hollywood glorifies of slitting wrists with a single, perfect cut from edge to edge. Whatever had been used to complete the act, she had been forced to hack into her flesh. Her pain—physical and emotional—must've been excruciating. Where one slice should have been there were instead numerous gashes. The layer of fat below her skin was bubbling up through the angry slashes creating murky white globules in a sea of red.

Her once soft, brown eyes were black with pain. Focused on something in the distance, it filled her with a dread I have never seen before…or since. I can only surmise she was facing eternity then, and it wasn't the cool, soft, inviting clouds of Heaven that she gazed upon. Her body quivered and shook in my arms as she struggled to stay wound in her mortal coil.

Her head rolled back allowing her wild eyes to

lock with mine. In that moment of loss and horror, I wanted her to call to me, to plead to be saved. I wanted her to apologize for having an affair and trying so desperately to leave me. I know it was selfish, but I needed some kind of release. Something...

Anything.

I would have taken any half-formed syllable of my name, but instead she spoke his. Her lips pursed and fell wide, his name tumbling from her tongue.

He had drawn her like a siren. His song was sweet, inviting, and must have seemed like a ray of hope in her dreary world. His winding, haunting melody spoke of sweet attention, and love—something she desperately craved. Running blindly through the fog, she was unable to realize her mistake until it was too late and was utterly dashed against the rocks. Her spirit was shattered and her heart was broken.

Many nights I would watch her watching me. I can still see her face, her big, brown eyes, her soft lips, and her raven-colored hair spilling down around her shoulders. And in those moments—those stretches of perfect silence—we found equilibrium and love. She was every bit my equal, my partner, but at the same time, she was above me. Her grasp on reality was much more substantial than mine, as she endeavored to keep my feet rooted firmly on the ground. If only I could have done the same for her...

Had I been there for Irene, had I taken notice of her emotional state, I could have acted. Instead I ignored her and allowed my wife to sink deeper into her pit of misery and despair. I was too wrapped up in my own life to be bothered with someone else's problems. In the end, it was my selfishness that cost my wife's life. I lost her to him, then I lost her entirely. In her time of need, I had abandoned her.

And I will never forgive myself for that.

As the glimmer of life slipped from her eyes, I knew her last thought had been of him even though she lay in my arms…and I was utterly crushed.

The white plastic phone slipped from my blood-soaked hand onto the floor and hit with a hollow crack that sent shivers down the back of my neck. I could hear the operator's voice still speaking to me, trying to calm me, and assuring me the ambulance was on its way. She was right. I could hear the faint cry of sirens growing slowly louder outside my—our—home. The first of the blue and red pulses of light shimmered across my front windows, but it was too late.

Irene was already gone.

My grief, my anger, and my pain overwhelmed me. Falling forward on her lifeless chest, I gasped and gagged as I cried. This woman who had just come back into my life, who I had promised to cherish and protect, was dead in my arms. I had failed her, and myself. Emotions chewed on my insides like torrents of acidic vomit. I couldn't stop it…

As I searched for her heartbeat, everything—every emotion, every thought, every pain—that I had experienced over the past six months rushed out of me like flood waters from a broken levee.

A pair of firm hands pressed against my

88

shoulders and started to lift me up. As another pair wrapped in thin, blue latex gloves began touching Irene, I freaked. Latching my arms around my dead wife, I pinned myself to her quickly cooling body frantically. The two men in white tried to pull us apart, but I wouldn't let go. She wasn't gone. I could feel it. There was some small spark of life left in this husk of a body and I would not relegate it to the ambulance crew. I only knew if they took her, she would be stripped and zipped into one of those horrible black body bags. I couldn't stand the thought of Irene alone, scared, or suffering within.

She wasn't dead!

As we scuffled about the floor, the emergency crew finally gained the upper hand. I felt a quick, sharp sting in my shoulder then the all-too-familiar chemical burn in my tissue. Snapping my head around, I saw one of the EMTs step back from me, the needle still in his hand. My senses dulled. I felt languid and weak. Suddenly filled with cement, my hands were heavy and easily pulled away from Irene's body. Crumbling back to the floor, I watched the ceiling spin as if it were burning into the atmosphere in a retrograde orbit. A few more seconds and I would be gone.

I twisted my head slightly to see them lifting Irene onto a nearby gurney. There was no rush to their motions. They already knew she was gone. The only thing they had to do was deliver her to the hospital so her time of death could be called.

As one of the EMTs started to cater to me and make sure I was okay, my eyes remained on Irene. I watched them slowly zip the heavy black bag up over her body.

As it neared her head, I saw Irene blink.

"Wait!" I shouted, my hand shooting toward her.

I tried to break free, but couldn't. Fading fast, my head reeled as the world was consumed by darkness.

Sitting up on the couch, I rubbed my hand down my face trying to force the sleep away. Despair clung to me like a blanket. As I swung my feet over the edge, I instantly doubled over in pain, both from my bruised back and the anguish caused by the dream. While wrapping my hands across my stomach, I fought the urge to wretch. I could still see Irene's face streaked with black tears. Taking a long, slow breath, I was up again and tried to compose myself.

The Hollow's octagonal family room loomed around me like a bad dream, an ouroboros, never ending or beginning. The warm light filtering in from the morning sun was starting to cool as the afternoon died. My eyes fell upon the burnt orange pill bottle sitting on the end table next to the couch. I glanced at the white label and read the dentist's name who had originally issued the prescription. Given to me after a vicious root canal, the Vicodin had seemed like a good idea for my aching back, however the medicine head that accompanied the pain relief proved differently.

With a strange familiarity that surprised me, I threw my arm over the back of the couch and rested my head. What felt very much like a hangover carpeted my brain and clogged my synapses. I was groggy and my limbs seemed to be encased in some sort of sticky goo. Trying to focus through blurred eyes, I stared at the mantle before me. "Stared" may have been too strong of a word. My vision merely settled on the mantle and I became incapable of looking away. I think I was stoned.

Jack…

I shot off the couch and was somehow instantly alert and completely cognizant of my surroundings. I scanned the living room. It was her. I swear to God it was Irene's voice.

The rhythmic thump of my heart filled my ears like tribal drums. "Hello?"

I waited.

Drawing in a quick breath, I held it and tried to quiet myself. The Hollow was almost perfectly quiet. I heard the sad howl of a dog in the distance.

There was no response, no sound at all.

Snatching my green flashlight off the coffee table where I had left it, I held it firmly in my fist. After quickly making my way to the foyer, I grabbed my laptop bag and dug my digital recorder from the front pocket. Setting the bag aside, I then powered up the device and started recording as swiftly as I could. Back into the family room, I walked around the octagonal walls but stopped in front of the coffee table. Daylight was fading and I felt no small amount of trepidation at facing my first night alone in the house.

"Is there anyone here?" I asked and lifted the recorder. "Would anyone like to speak to me?"

Asking questions could sometimes stimulate electronic voice phenomenon. The recorder somehow captured answers I was unable to hear at the time. These were standard questions proven to produce results. Still, it was at best hit or miss. There was no exact way to get EVPs, and I wouldn't know if anything had been captured until I reviewed the tape. And rule number one was to never stop recording. I was tossing darts at a bull's eye in the middle of the night with no hope of seeing where they hit. It seemed the departed just wanted someone to talk to.

"Am I intruding in your home?" I paused. "Do you not want me here?"

There was no answer. I heard the pipes in the old house creak, but nothing more. I let the recorder fall to my side in frustration. I sighed. I didn't think I was going to get anything.

Jack, the window...

I jumped.

Not more than a whisper, but I heard it as if it had been uttered right into my ear. It was her. I knew it without a shadow of a doubt. Spinning, I scanned the room frantically. I was alone, utterly and completely. My heart was pounding again like a heavy metal drum solo.

"Irene," I said her name. It sounded strange, almost alien, as it rolled off my tongue. It had been rattling around in my brain ever since her death, but I hadn't had the courage to say it aloud. "Please talk to me," I begged. My eyes jumped randomly between the eight walls, searching for anything. "I need you."

I waited, but the old house only groaned. Slumping onto the couch, I felt defeated.

"Electronic voice phenomenon isn't real."

I shot up for a third time and spun wildly almost crashing into the coffee table. I knew this voice too, and a deep darkness settled in my chest. Somehow keeping my balance, my eyes fell upon the evil marionette. Tossed on the foyer stairs like a favorite doll that had been inadvertently discarded, her long, slender limbs lolled languidly away from her body. Wednesday's lips curled ever so slightly into a smile, and would have been easily missed if I weren't glaring. If my eyes could shoot laser beams, she would already have been a charred, smoking corpse.

"It's all in your head," Wednesday said. "You're hearing what you want to hear in the pops and static, creating something to desperately hold on to your guilt."

After dropping the recorder on the coffee table, I started toward the foyer but kept a safe distance. "What are you doing in my home? I'll call the cops if you don't leave right now."

"Your home?" she asked mockingly. "You can't own The Hollow."

"I can," I corrected, "because I'm not a penniless freak like you."

Her smile contorted into a harsh frown that seemed to drop the corners of her mouth off her face. "That wasn't beautiful, Jack," she whimpered, "but I didn't come here to fight." Wednesday brought her hand up and pulled it slowly through her raven hair. Wrapping it around her fingertips, she twirled it playfully, almost seductively.

Holding my flashlight like a weapon, I took a

measured step into the foyer. My mind was swimming with questions, but only one surfaced and became completely realized. "Why are you doing this to me?"

Wednesday's hurt faded, replaced by that wicked grin I had come to know so well...and hate. "I'm here to help."

Somewhere in the deep recesses of my brain, I imagined myself rushing across the floor, pinning her down, and bludgeoning her to death with my flashlight. Feeling her imaginary blood splatter on my face, I shook my head and pulled myself back to reality. "I want you out of my house right now."

A flicker of disgust crossed her face as if she knew what I was thinking—which wouldn't surprise me at all. The hem of the long, black skirt she wore was hiked up slightly, revealing the fishnet stockings that raced down her curvy legs and disappeared into her chunky boots.

I was both repelled and oddly enthralled by the sight.

Wednesday cocked her eyebrow curiously. "You would throw away my offer of assistance so quickly?"

"I don't want anything from you," I said. "Wait," I corrected myself, "I do want one thing."

The marionette tilted her head. "And that would be...?"

I returned her evil grin. "I want you to get the fuck out of my house!"

Wednesday lifted her arms and yanked her body angrily into a sitting position while her face contorted into a sneer. "I come to you with no pretense, no demands," she said, "and yet you constantly mock and abuse me. What is your problem?"

"My problem?" I asked in awe of the question. "My problem? What the hell are you talking about? You stalk me, break into my home, and God knows how, but you have intimate details about my life. You're really starting to freak me out, Wednesday." I paused and stared malevolently at the evil marionette, sizing her up. I wanted to hurt her, but I wasn't sure how. Then it came to me, a bolt out of the blue. "The only problem I have," I concluded, "is you."

Her eyes widened and her expression was as if I had just slapped her hard across the face. Her body was perfectly still in horror. I couldn't even tell if she was breathing. After a long moment, she collected her limbs and stood. Dragging a wayward lock of hair from her face with her slender pinky, Wednesday slowly turned and started up the stairs.

"Wait," I took a step closer to the stairs. "Where are you going?" I pointed my thumb over my shoulder. "The door's over there. Wednesday?"

She hit the landing, turned, and continued toward the second floor.

Climbing onto the first step with my hand clasped firmly to the rail, I refused to continue upwards. As if to remind me of the earlier incident, my lower back pulsed with pain. The Vicodin felt like it was chewing through my stomach and intestines, and the urge to wretch was growing quickly. I craned my head to follow Wednesday until her legs disappeared from sight. I took another tentative step. "Wednesday?"

Finally reaching the landing, I tried to fight back the overwhelming sense of dread that settled over me. My hand throbbed as I gripped the flashlight tightly in fear.

I turned…

…and found nothing.

Wednesday was gone. Completely. My sense of curiosity overwhelmed the fear momentarily and compelled me to the top. Remembering my last encounter, I moved cautiously away from the stairs. Scanning down the hallway, I could see it was bereft and silent. A large window at the end framed the branches of an old oak tree swaying gently in the wind. A shrill squeak slithered down the hall as the tree's wooden fingers scraped against the pane of glass. The sound assaulted my flesh, raising goose bumps and sent chills down my extremities.

Unlike the first, the second floor was unfurnished. Either the previous occupants hadn't come up here—after my earlier encounter I could certainly understand why—or the real estate company had only left the furniture downstairs to help sell the home. Dust settled on the hardwood floor allowing me to clearly see my footprints from earlier, but the rest of the hall remained untouched. Outlines of missing decorations were permanently pressed into the dusty walls like the shadows of victims of the Hiroshima blast. Directly behind the stairwell, the shape of a crucifix gave me the shivers. Three heavy gashes ripped through the faded outline like claw marks from a wild animal, and a big one at that. As my eyes scanned the empty hallway, fear burned and sizzled inside of me like acid. Three doors stood silently in the walls, one on the right, two on the left. On the opposite side of the stairs, the pattern was repeated. With no idea what lived behind the doors, I considered each uncomfortably.

"Wednesday?" My voice was thin, weakened by fear, but I had to know. She had to be here.

My stomach grumbled and felt as though it were doing gymnastics. I knew vomit wasn't far behind. Doing my best to chew it back, I chose a door at random. Leaving the safety of the banister, I watched my shoes make scuff marks in the dust. There's no way Wednesday could've come this way and not left a trail. I just couldn't wrap my mind around the idea. As my mind attempted to puzzle it out, I reached for the doorknob.

Get away!

I ripped my hand away from the knob like it had been burned. The warning came from a female, but that was all I could discern. It was low and harsh, almost angry. I cradled the flesh of my hand as if it were wounded. The twisting ball of snakes in my gut was becoming angrier. After snapping my head up, I frantically searched the hallway again.

I was alone.

My curiosity overwhelmed me, and I prayed quickly I hadn't become the cat. Swallowing hard, I turned my attention back to the door and settled it on the round, gold handle. Reaching down, my fingers hovered nervously mere centimeters from the knob. My hand was beginning to shake. I perked my ears listening for the voice again, but the house remained quiet. A knot welled up in my throat threatening to choke me, but I had to know. Grabbing the knob, I paused and waited. Pulling in a sharp breath, I twisted and heard the mechanism disengage with a loud click.

The air around me became dense and still and felt cold as though the temperature had dropped several degrees. "Crap." I sighed, already aware of what was coming.

The door flew open and knocked me on my ass.

Stars sparkled before my eyes as my head snapped back and cracked against the wall. Pounding footfalls, rumbling like the sound of thunder, became the focus of my attention. Struggling through my blurred vision, I stared oddly up a long staircase through the open doorway. The stairs looked old, steep, and rickety. Cracks spread across the thin, rotting wood and looked like it would give if any weight were placed on it, yet I could hear something coming down. They creaked and popped as the booming steps grew closer. I swear that I thought it was the Devil himself coming to claim me.

Boom…another step.

Cold sweat rolled down my face as my heart thumped wildly in my ears. I craned my head down, but couldn't see the top. It was as though the steps rose and were swallowed by darkness. I froze. Every muscle in my body locked up and refused to act.

Boom…boom!

I shivered. My skin crawled like it was trying to escape my body. It sounded as though it was right on top of me, but I still couldn't see anything. The doorway stood empty and there was nothing on the stairs.

Boom!

Pure terror blossomed like a nuclear furnace in my chest and forced me against the wall. Suddenly on my feet, I felt my nails dig into the hard wood as I tried to claw a hole to escape through. Unable to look away from the door, I didn't see the smear of blood I was creating as my fingertips shredded against the wall.

Jack, run!

I shot away from the wall like a missile and slammed the door closed with the full force of my body. I wasn't thinking, but acting on pure adrenaline alone. Bouncing and twisting like a linebacker throwing off a tackle, I sprinted away then angled down the stairs. I wasn't sure if my feet touched the ground as I swung over the middle landing. One of the sentry ferns tumbled as my flailing hand snagged a leaf.

Once I reached the bottom, I stopped. Spinning on my heels, my eyes snapped to the top of the stairs. My chest heaved as I caught my breath, and I tried to slow my racing heart. I stood motionless, waiting and listening. The Hollow was completely silent. I could feel the front door staring into my back. It waited patiently, full expecting to be used. I backpedaled once, but stopped. I wasn't going to leave. Only then did it register that a female voice told me to run...and it sounded very much like Irene's.

What the hell was going on in this house? It

occurred to me for a moment that I may still be asleep from the pain medication, but I dismissed the idea as idiotic. I sincerely hoped I wasn't pulling a Dallas. Maybe I should go check the shower for Bobby. I rubbed my fingers over my brow and caught sight of my bloody fingertips for the first time. Several of my nails were cracked or broken, and my flesh was peeled back angrily. Dark blood streaked back over my hands. I wasn't certain if a hospital visit was in order, but I knew this was a little beyond Johnson & Johnson's scope.

I took a slow, deep breath and finally felt my pounding heart begin to ease. Then a knock on the front door scared the hell out of me.

Chapter Eleven

I stared at the front door as if it were some sort of mysterious alien artifact. Was I waiting for it to magically open, or reveal to me the identity of the person on the other side? Was there even anyone there or was the house messing with me again? I leveled the patented Devlin stink-eye at the stairs, just in case. That would show this house who the boss was. Uh huh, sure, Jack... I was about as threatening as a three-legged mouse.

Moving to the door, I wrapped my bloody hand around the knob but paused, unsure if I should actually open it. I started to twist, but was met with resistance. Thinking that the blood on my hands may be hindering me, I wiped them quickly on my jeans and tried again. Gritting my teeth, I clenched down on the knob and used all of my force, but it didn't budge.

"Come on!" I shouted in exasperation as I took a step back. It was starting to get to me.

I heard an unfamiliar, muffled voice on the other side of the door. I held my place, nervously waiting until I heard it again. Moving back to the door, I pressed my ear to the wood and held my breath. A moment passed before I softly called out. To my amazement, and the possible salvation of my sanity, there came a reply. I pounded my fists on the door and informed the person to wait while I tried to open it. I wasn't sure how stupid that sounded, but I didn't care. I had to see another living person right now. I needed it. I would get this door open even if it meant leveling the entire house to do so.

As though the house received the threat, I heard the bolt disengage. Cocking my head slightly, I stepped back and watched the door swing open under its own power.

"What the hell is going on?"

My eyes settled on the large, Hispanic woman standing on my front porch. I recognized her from the piano bar at the hotel, and remembered the card she had dropped during her hasty exit. "Angel Arroyo?"

She nodded. "Yes." I saw the spark of recognition in her eyes as well. "You're the nut from the bar."

Nut from the bar... My P.R. agent was hard at work. Obviously the greeting didn't sit well with me. Was that really how people perceived me? "Uh, yeah," I breathed. "What are you doing at my home?"

She pointed over her shoulder at a tan coupe parked horribly by the curb. "I got a flat. I don't have a cell so I came here to see if I could use your phone. I had no idea you lived here."

"Or you would've chosen a different house?" I finished her thought.

She nodded.

"Well I don't have a landline," I dug my hand into my pocket and produced my slender, black cell phone, "but you're welcome to use this."

"Oh my God," she gasped. "What happened to your hand?"

Damn. I forgot. How the hell was I going to explain this?

102

"We need to get your hand taken care of." Angel took my hand and stepped into the house.

As soon as she crossed the threshold, a dark shadow passed over her face and her eyes rolled back. As though being electrocuted, her body shivered and convulsed. I panicked, thinking for sure the black entity had her. Grabbing her meaty arm, I spun and tried to maneuver her back through the door. I pushed, but her feet were firmly fixed in place.

"Ms. Arroyo," I said almost frantically as I tried to budge her. "Hello?"

There was no response to my shouts. The whites of her eyes showed through her fluttering eyelids. You know those toys that dance and wobble wildly when you press the button in the base? Yeah. She looked exactly like one of those. Twisting back at her knees, her torso spun and her arms flipped wildly around. Unable to dodge quickly enough, one of her massive paws swung over and smashed me down. Hitting the floor like a sack of shit, my already bruised and battered body screamed in pain. This was fun.

Lifting my head, I watched Angel spread her arms and rise off the floor as if gripped by some massive hand. She looked less like her namesake and more like a side of beef hanging from a hook. I heard her gag as she tried to draw breath and her olive skin had taken on a very definite tint of blue. Trying to lift my damaged body up to help, I saw her convulse one final time then fall forward.

Angel hit the floor with a resounding smack and was suddenly very, very still.

Dragging myself toward her, I started to reach out a hand but stopped. Visions of Irene dying in my arms flashed through my mind and I recoiled. Fighting the ghost in my head, I moved my shaking hand tentatively toward her flesh. Touching her throat, I was shocked at its coolness. Staring at the back of her head, I ran my fingertips around to her windpipe and searched for her pulse. Digging my fingers into the meat of her neck, I found a steady beat. It throbbed powerfully beneath my fingertips and offered me some relief. She wasn't dead, or dying.

Rolling onto my back, I snatched my discarded cell phone from the floor and flipped it open. The screen flickered twice, probably because of the impact, but finally came to life. I tapped my fingers against the smooth, plastic buttons, inputting the familiar three-digit emergency number. Drawing a breath before I hit send, I needed a moment to calm myself.

I felt a hand grab my arm.

Almost jumping out of my skin, I shot up off the floor faster than I knew I could. With my back pressed to the wall of the foyer, I watched Angel struggle to get onto her side.

"Ms. Arroyo?" I asked, carefully walking toward her. She didn't respond. After what she had just been through, I wasn't completely shocked. I stopped, still holding my phone tightly in my hand, and my thumb hovering over the send button. "Angel?"

Drawing up onto her hands and knees, she shook her head like a dog that had just been beaten.

Her jet black hair spilled down and pooled on the floor. Drawing her hands back, she sat up on her legs as though deep in prayer. Eyes still closed, I watched her pull a breath in through her nose and slowly exhale through her mouth.

I held my position, unsure what to do. I seriously considered dialing 9-1-1, but an attack by a ghost didn't quite seem to fit the nature of the service.

"Oy," Angel breathed finally. "That was a big one."

I waited.

She opened her eyes and fixed a scowl on me. "You're not even going to offer to help me up?"

I jumped toward her as though slapped on the ass, all the while issuing an apology.

Wrapping her sausagelike fingers around my hand, I marveled for a moment at how small mine looked against hers. It wasn't that she was ugly—far from it actually—there was just a lot of her to love (not that it's always a bad thing). I would say that Angel was classically beautiful. Her facial features, although large, were nearly perfect and her gorgeous, lush eyes were open windows into her soul. As she struggled to her feet, I noted the exhaustion in her face for the first time. Had it been there all along?

"Are you okay?" I asked finally.

"Do I look like I'm okay?" she spat out as she dusted off her black slacks and adjusted her jacket. "I just got mugged by a pissed-off ghost. How do you think I feel, jackass?"

"Uh...sorry," was all I could stammer in reply.

At least I had an idea what I had just witnessed. "A ghost did that to you?"

"No, cabrón," Angel said. "I magically floated in the air and choked myself. I'll be appearing with David Copperfield and Harry Houdini in my next televised magic show."

She was a feisty one! "I'd watch that," I answered with a smirk. "Can I get you something?"

The paranormal investigator sighed. "A glass of water maybe?"

I took a step back, but stopped. After what I had just witnessed, I wasn't sure I wanted to go anywhere in this house alone. "This kitchen's around the corner," I said slyly, trying not to let her see my fear.

She nodded and followed me with a slight limp.

I turned and started past the stairs. This was becoming more and more surreal by the moment. Walking around the corner, I cradled my ribs. Stars sparkled in front of my eyes for a moment as pain coursed through my body, but I somehow managed to hold it together. My head swam as I thought about what I had just seen, and events earlier today.

This all seemed so…familiar. I couldn't explain why.

Chapter Twelve

As Angel and I sat at the small kitchen table, I recounted everything—everything—that had led me to Union and The Hollow. I spoke candidly about Irene and her death for the first time in almost a year. It probably helped that this was a total stranger sitting across from me, but there was something warm and trusting about this woman. She struck me as very motherly. I didn't expect her to give me a hug and a cookie, but I wasn't sure it was out of the realm of possibilities. Maybe I just had to ask. I glanced up into her face...or maybe not.

I spun my glass slowly on the table watching the remaining water slosh messily about the bottom. "So that's it," I said to break the silence that had settled between us.

"Quite a story," Angel said. She took a moment to process it. I could see the gears churning behind her eyes. "So you've been seeking out every haunted house you can in hopes of somehow making contact with your dead wife?"

The revelation was shocking, to me at least. I knew what I was doing, but hearing what my life had become summarized into a twenty word sentence seemed so stark and raw. I honestly had no idea how to reply to that question. There was no answer I could give Angel that wouldn't make me sound like a raving lunatic. Which, in retrospect, I probably was.

Angel finished her glass of water and set it aside. "What are you trying to achieve by this? Are you hoping to make peace with her?"

I shrugged. "I'm not entirely sure. I just need—" I stopped. Why was it that I was always using the words "I" and "need" when talking about Irene? Was this about her…or me? I was seriously starting to not like who I had become.

And why did I have a serious case of déjà vu nagging me? This all seemed so familiar…but I couldn't peg why.

"I'm not sure what I need," I admitted. At least that much was the truth. I wanted to change the subject. "What happened out there? I mean, really?"

"I'm what's called a Conduit," Angel answered. "I have latent psychic abilities, but can't express them myself. Spirits, however, can use me to talk or act on their behalf."

I had heard the term before, but never really stopped to consider how frightening the possibility was. Here was a woman whose body could be taken over at any time, and she really had no say in the matter. Why she didn't live in a concrete bunker somewhere deep underground was beyond my reasoning.

"The Spirit in this house tried to take me over," Angel confirmed, "but I fought it."

I cocked an eyebrow. "You can do that?"

She nodded. "It's taken a long time, and a great amount of concentration to learn, but I do have some control over it now. When I felt it enter me in the foyer, I knew I couldn't let it take over. It's very angry." She paused. "Mostly at you for some reason."

I sat back uncomfortably in my chair. "Me?" I

had the overwhelming urge to get up, and run screaming from the house right now. "What did I do?"

"I don't know," Angel said. "All I could sense was pure rage. And it was directed completely at you."

Neat.

"Why doesn't it just kill me then?"

"No Idea." Angel shrugged. "Cat and mouse mean anything to you?"

Again: neat.

Then there was the burning question. "Who is it?"

"That," Angel said and took a long, deep breath, "I don't know. There were only feelings, no identity."

"Doesn't really help me." I rubbed my fingers over my furrowed brow.

"I can only tell you what I felt," she replied unapologetically. "But I know this thing was trying to use me," she lifted her face and locked eyes with me, "to kill you."

I had the sudden urge to hide all the sharp implements in the house and ask Angel to leave. Or maybe I should just leave. That seemed like the sensible thing to do. Closing my eyes, I tried to process all of this new information. "What do I do?"

"Leave," Angel's advice echoed my inner voice.

"I can't."

"You're an idiot," she surmised. "You need to get out of this house right now. Stand up," she pointed toward the front door, "and leave. Right now."

She didn't understand. I shook my head. "I can't. This could be my only chance."

"Leave right now," she reiterated forcefully.

I leaned back in my chair and leveled my gaze at her. My mind was made up. "No."

The paranormal investigator nodded and stood. "Then you are going to die," Angel stated unemotionally. She glanced at me one more time then started for the front door. She had nothing left to say.

I wanted to let her storm out of the house on her high horse, but… "Wait."

Just beyond the kitchen door, she stopped and waited but didn't turn.

"I need you," I admitted.

"What you need is to get out of this house," she said bluntly. "Go back to wherever you're from and forget about Union and The Hollow."

"I'll pay you," I offered.

"Get out of here, Jack," Angel said undeterred.

I listened to her warning, but didn't budge. I wasn't leaving, and neither was she. I needed her help if I wanted to contact Irene. "I'll double your usual rate."

"I don't want your money," she said almost angrily. "Don't you understand?" she asked, still only offering me her back. "The spirit—if it even is a human spirit—could use me to kill you. This thing hates you, Jack. I don't know why, and I'm not sure I want to know. Pack up your things and go…while you still can."

I shifted in my seat for a moment. "Triple."

Angel paused, took a breath, and turned. "Okay. Where do we start?"

Chapter Thirteen

Angel wasted no time in calling in her team of investigators, and despite the late hour, they showed up ready for work. The four person team, each with their own special area of interest and expertise, quickly went to work canvassing The Hollow with equipment. A mixture of occult and top-of-the-line tech, the equipment was designed to measure and document the activity. I was surprised, and reassured, by their professionalism. Barking orders like a drill sergeant, Angel presided over the set up with cool efficiency. I tried to help as much as I could, but was mostly relegated to getting out of the way.

I was introduced to each of Angel's team.

Jared, a redheaded twenty-something who was attempting to grow a beard despite his Scottish heritage, was an eccentric Wiccan who didn't quite seem to fit the mold. I had expected a slightly overweight girl who kept wishing me "peace and blessings," all the while discussing her menstrual cycle. Jared was cool and collected, and appeared highly attuned with the energies surrounding him. Clad in fashionably worn jeans, Chucks, and a t-shirt, he wore a black ceremonial robe over them that billowed as he walked. At least he wasn't skyclad. He seemed to have a very definable calming effect on those around him. It was nice to have him here, as he brought a sense of tranquility to the madness.

And then there was Singe. How she had come

to own that particular nickname I wasn't entirely sure, but it could have something to do with the barely visible burn scars peeking out from the collar of her shirt. Like me, she was an audiophile. She covered the house with digital recorders, and set up a mobile workstation in the family room with the most impressive digital audio manipulation software I had ever seen. Her blond hair was cut into a trendy bob, with the bottom layers died black. She wasn't beautiful, but not hard on the eyes either. And true to her specialty, Singe listened. I hadn't heard her speak more than a few sentences during her time in The Hollow. She had already expressed interest in listening to my EVPs, and reviewing the recording I had made earlier.

With so many video cameras it would have made NBC jealous, Brad was the video specialist. Using the same high-end digital cameras that some Hollywood directors had adopted to film with, it was obvious he had money. After talking with him, I learned he owned and operated an advertising agency in the greater New York area, which explained where the cameras and money came from. Fairly nondescript, Brad was the kind of person you would pass on the street and never look twice at. He was taller than me with mousy brown hair, and a tuft of hair on his chin. A few gray hairs had started peeking through, but they didn't detract from his youthful face. Probably not more than his mid-thirties, I really couldn't peg his age.

And finally, there was Jasmine, but everyone called her "Jazz." Her beautiful light brown hair and chocolate skin set off her powerful blue eyes. She looked more like a model than a paranormal investigator, except she was too curvy. She had fantastic hips, and breasts that seemed to somehow give her supernatural powers. Like Angel, Jazz was a psychic conduit, and from little hints dropped during conversation, was even more acutely tuned than Angel. She kept a black crystal slung around her neck, barely dangling above her cleavage, that she said protected her from negative energy. She was gorgeous, but had an air of power around her. I was glad she was on our side. At least, I thought with a smirk, for the time being.

I wandered slowly through The Hollow watching each of them work. Brad was trying to cover the stairs and second floor with as many angles as he could, and seemed genuinely excited by the prospect of capturing a ghost. Obviously he hadn't been thrown down the stairs yet. Jared, in his big, black robe, had set up a makeshift altar in the kitchen and had been calling us in one by one to bless us with smoke from burning sage and holy water. Singe and Jazz were running cables for the few wired microphones Singe had set up back to her compact, eight channel mixer in the octagonal living room. As they unwound the thick cables, they used gaffer's tape to keep them against the baseboards.

Each was trying their best to hide it, but I saw the shifting eyes, and the nervous glances behind them as they worked. Each had lived in the area long enough to hear at least one story about The Hollow, and all had been briefed on my and Angel's personal experiences. Just below the light, jovial conversation of the setting up, I could feel their tension gradually stretching like a rubber band. I couldn't blame them. Angel hadn't, thankfully, revealed my ultimate goal here. She had instead simply told them that I had just moved here and wanted the house investigated. I wasn't sure how they would react if they found out I had sought out this house, and had somehow provoked the spirit within in an attempt to contact my deceased wife. Every time I said it, it just seemed that much more insane.

What the hell was I doing…?

I stopped in the foyer and glanced up to see Singe and Jazz running cable down the edge of the stairs. Jazz was kneeling down and I spotted the purple arches of her thong peeking out above her low-riding jeans. Immediately feeling like a dirty old man, I wanted to turn away, but didn't. I imagined her for a moment in something from Victoria's Secret, or better yet, Frederick's of Hollywood and felt that familiar tingling downstairs. It had been a long time since I let my mind wander there, and while it wasn't entirely unpleasant, it felt wrong. Here I was trying to contact my dead wife, and fantasizing about another woman. I pulled my eyes away from Jazz and let them fall shamefully to the floorboards like a schoolboy who had been caught reading those "special" editions of National Geographic.

"You okay?"

I brought my guilty eyes up to meet Angel's gaze.

She craned her head back like a bird's at my

expression of guilt. I don't think that was what she was expecting to see.

"Yeah," I said, "just tired."

She nodded. "It is almost two in the morning. What time is it where you're from?"

I thought for a moment, doing the time zone conversion in my head. "Not quite midnight." My mind wandered back to my spacious home in Southern Idaho, and my comfortable bed.

"If you want to go get some rest, feel free," Angel offered. "We have things covered here for the time being."

I wrapped my hand around my bruised ribs and finally nodded. "Thank you. If you need anything…"

"I promise we'll wake you," Angel finished. "It might be wise if we all slept in the same room tonight. Entities tend to single people out before they attack."

I really didn't want to sleep in the same room with these people, especially Jazz. I had no doubt she had a slinky set of pajamas she would change into and then suddenly have to go running around the house with her boobs bouncing, like in all the horror movies. I shook my head and tried to wipe the exhaustion from my face. I was tired. "I'll be okay," I assured her. "Besides, it's probably better if I don't sleep too near two conduits tonight." I smiled. "Just in case."

Angel chuckled. "Good point. Sleep well."

"Thanks." Reluctantly turning away, I headed down the same hallway to the right of the stairs that led to the kitchen and dining room. Beyond them

116

were the first floor bedroom and the study. Glancing into the kitchen as I passed, I saw Jared mixing a concoction as strands of smoke weaved up and around him. I had never really seen a Wiccan work magic, though I had written about it in a book. I thought about stopping for a moment and asking if I could just watch, but I wasn't sure if I would disturb him, and I really needed to rest. The Vicoden was sitting like a rock in my gut, and the medicine hangover was just starting to abate. I needed sleep.

Reaching the end of the hallway, I turned right toward the master bedroom and opened the door. Feeling blindly up the wall for the light switch, I finally found it and flicked it on. Like the rest of the first floor rooms, the master bedroom was decorated completely and lavishly. A four-poster bed reached out from the far wall, covered with a rich brown, white, and black comforter and numerous pillows. An oddly creepy bearskin rug occupied the floor between the door and the bed, with its mouth pulled open into a perpetual growl showing off its powerful teeth. The dead grizzly's eyes glistened beneath the lights and almost looked alive. Almost.

Moving around the rug, and careful not to step on it, I stopped and stared at a huge painting that stretched across most of the wall to the bed's right. Not of anything specific that I could determine, dark lines spun across the canvas and curled around each other while minimal, subdued swatches of color highlighted and vanished into themselves. The design seemed to weave in and out of itself, never truly beginning or ending. I wondered for a moment if I stared at it long enough, if an image would appear like those 3D posters popular in the '90s. I bet it was a boat. It was beautiful in a strange way, but didn't seem to fit the design of the rest of The Hollow. It was very modern, while the rest of the home was firmly rooted in the '30s and '40s.

Turning away, I spotted my suitcase I had deposited here earlier. After peeling off my shirt, I tossed it in a pile on the corner of the huge, king-sized bed. After hoisting my suitcase up, I unzipped the top and lifted it open. My manuscript, the one James had verbally shredded, stared helplessly at me as though it was a puppy I had been neglecting. I didn't need its abuse right now. I had a whole house dying to abuse me. Snatching the manuscript up, I proceeded to set it on the bed next to my discarded shirt. I started to turn back to my clothes, but I felt it staring at me. Far from the parental emotions I experienced during its rescue, James' words were starting to get to me. What was worse, I knew somewhere in the back of my head that he might be right. I had been so focused on ghost hunting, I had churned out a chunk of crap just to satisfy my publishing contract. I pinched the bridge of my nose for a moment and tried to ignore it, but it wasn't working. It was a good book, but it was beginning to feel like a failure. Grabbing the stack of papers, I flipped it face down in my arms and stuffed it into the top drawer of the nightstand next to the bed. Out of sight, out of mind…right? Or would it become Poe's Tell-Tale Heart?

Digging past the various jeans and haphazardly folded pairs of underwear, I freed a black and brown pair of pajama bottoms. Undoing my belt and opening the top button of my jeans, I spun and sat on the edge of the bed. I suddenly felt uncomfortable as if being watched. I searched the room, but saw nothing. My eyes stopped on the painting and a strange feeling settled over me. It looked as though it had changed. The pattern was somehow slightly different…wasn't it? Or maybe I was overtired and imagining it? The urge to jump under the sheets and pull them up over my head like a child gripped me. Fighting it off, I stood up and unzipped. I wasn't going to let this place control me. I was here for a reason. I didn't give a rat's ass what it wanted. Don't fear the Reaper, baby. After dropping my jeans and shorts, I stepped out of them and snatched my pajamas. After pulling them on, I closed my suitcase and deposited it back on the floor.

Before making my way across the room to turn off the overhead light, I snapped on the small lamp by the bedside. I wasn't scared, I assured myself, I just didn't want to trip over something. After making my way around the bearskin, I flicked off the light and headed back to bed. Once I pulled down the comforter and sheet, I pushed a few of the decorative pillows out of the way. Scooting in, I wondered when the last time the sheets were cleaned, or when someone actually slept here. Not that it concerned me too deeply because my eyelids started to feel heavy as soon as I settled in. Pulling the blankets up to my chin, I exhaled slowly trying to settle my nerves. I felt a good, stiff drink would do a better job, but wasn't sure how it would react to the leftover painkillers in my system. I could hear the muffled voices of Angel and her team outside, and it brought me some comfort. At least if anything happened, they would be here.

After snapping off the light, I rolled onto my side and wrapped the blankets around me like a warm tortilla. Comfortably burritoed, I closed my eyes and let my mind drift. I wandered first back to Jazz and my earlier fantasy, but quickly turned to Irene. I saw her face and body covered in blood, but forcefully changed the thought to a happier occasion: our first anniversary in Hawaii. We walked slowly, silently down the moonlit beaches hand in hand. It sounds cliché, but it was absolutely perfect. The warm waves lapped at our feet, and the moonlight sparkled off the millions of ripples on the clear, perfect Pacific Ocean. We didn't say much because nothing needed to be said. We just walked, enjoyed each other, and the night. That was back when we were truly in love, before she had lost herself, and I stopped caring.

My eyes popped open at the revelation. As I stared into the darkness, I realized I had stopped caring. I had taken for granted that she would always be there to care for and love me and I had stopped reciprocating. I had stopped taking care of her. But I already knew that, didn't I? It was why I was here.

I felt something slide up my inner thigh. "Not quite a rocket scientist, are you?"

Before I even realized what I was doing, terror had propelled me up out of the bed and pinned me against the wall. As my eyes adjusted to the darkness, I saw the shape of a body in the bed. My heart pounding, I couldn't help but stare. I started to make out facial features and my racing heart began to slow, although I wasn't sure why. "This has gone way past the point of reason," I said angrily. "I want you out of my house right now, Wednesday."

She smiled at me from beneath the covers. Obviously naked, her arm stretched languidly across her breasts, hiding her nipples. "You still don't get it, Jack. This isn't your house. The Hollow doesn't belong to anyone. Especially you." She moved her arm playfully, but kept her private areas covered. She suddenly seemed better endowed than I remembered. "Jack, I'm here to help. I'm not going to hurt you." She smiled softly. "I promise."

I don't know why, but her words put me at a strangely uncomfortable ease.

I walked toward her and sat on the edge of the bed, still a comfortable distance away. "How do you keep getting into my house?"

"That's not important right now." She smirked.

"It kind of is to me," I retorted.

Grabbing the covers, Wednesday pulled them over her porcelain flesh and rolled onto her back. Sliding a hand behind her head and propping up a pillow, she looked completely relaxed like someone who had just experienced really fulfilling and exhausting sex. She was only missing the cigarette dangling dangerously in her hand. "Have you ever wondered about the end?"

"Seems I'm fairly preoccupied with it," I said.

She nodded and brushed a strand of black hair away from her blue eyes. "Good point. But I mean seriously, what happens to those we lose? Is there a

Heaven and Hell? And if so, who decides where we end up?"

"Wednesday." I sighed. "While this philosophical discussion is fascinating, I really don't have time for this. I have a group of ghost hunters in the house waiting to get to work, and I need sleep. Can you just be your usual cryptic self, make whatever point you came here to make, and go?"

"I'm hurt." She frowned deeply. "I keep coming to you offering to help, and you keep blowing me off. I'm going to stop offering soon."

That was fine by me. I drew a breath, searched for words to make a point, but let the air rush out in an exhausted sigh. I had nothing.

Wednesday pulled the covers down on my side. "Why don't you come to bed, Jack?"

I stared in awe. "Are you serious?"

She laughed. "I didn't say I was going to pounce on you, big boy. Settle down, Tiger."

I blushed and felt a sudden surge of anger. "Wednesday, you need to leave. Right now!"

"Fucking society." She threw off the covers and stood up in a huff. I caught a glimpse of her completely naked body, but turned away out of modesty. "A woman shows a hint of sexual independence and she's smacked down. That's bullshit, Jack."

"I thought you said you didn't want me," I said, staring at the floor. I waited for a response. "Wednesday?" I turned and glanced over my shoulder in time to see a flash of her naked backside before the bedroom door slammed shut. Did she really just walk into the foyer completely naked?

No way.

Pulling on my shirt, I ran to the door nearly tripping over the bear rug's head. Using the handle to save myself, I then threw open the door and rushed out. I could hear voices near the stairs. Bursting out of the hallway in my bare feet, I spotted Angel and squeaked to a stop. "Hey!"

Angel snapped her attention away from Singe to me. "Hey to you too, Jack."

I shook my head and waved my arms. "Did a naked woman just come through here? About this tall," I said, holding my hand to my chin, "black and purple hair. Looks like Wednesday Addams? And did I mention she was completely naked?"

Angel turned from me to Singe with an odd grin on her face. Singe shrugged, obviously missing the joke as well.

"I am not kidding," I barked. "She was just in my room!"

"No," Angel said. "No naked women here."

Singe laughed. "Nope. Just Jared, but we make him wear a sock now."

"This isn't funny!" I rubbed my hands over my face. I was dreaming. I had to be. "She was right in my room! She just came out here. I swear to God!"

"I'm sorry," Angel said, taking on a softer tone. "There hasn't been anyone in the house but us. I've been here in the foyer since you went to bed, and I didn't see anything. Plus, Brad has his video up and running," she added, trying to ease my fears. "If anyone was in the house, he would have alerted us."

There was an obvious hole in her reasoning.

"Do you have a camera in my room?"

"Of course," Angel stated so seriously that it frightened me.

I was losing my mind.

Well, that explained the feeling of being watched. "I want to see the tape right now."

Angel lifted a small, black radio to her mouth, "Brad, please tell me you have the video workstation up." She thumbed the talk button and turned away as she alerted the nearby team members to what was going on. We were on the move before she had even finished issuing orders. Brad responded that he would be ready when we arrived.

Moving up the hallway, we passed the kitchen where Jared was still incanting and headed directly for the study. The team had decided that would be the best location to operate the video equipment since it was basically central to the house. Pushing through the open door, I saw a maze of black cables snaking across the floor toward an impressive stack of recording and editing equipment piled on the antique desk that resided in the center. Shelves of books surrounded us, most of the titles I had never heard of. I wondered if the history of The Hollow was contained within this collection. I would have to look tomorrow.

Brad appeared from behind the equipment with a small videotape raised triumphantly in his hand. "I had just set up one of the older Hi-8s in Jack's room before he went in."

"Good work," Angel said with a nod. "Let's take a look."

124

Sliding into the matching antique chair, Brad rubbed his goatee as he inserted and queued up the tape. His fingers flew with confidence and familiarity over the various controls. He pointed up to the middle flat panel display he had arranged in a semi-circle before him. "Look here."

The monitor flickered once as Brad selected it on the mixing board before him. Hitting play, we watched a recording of Brad slowly backing away from the camera and peering at it to make sure he had set it up correctly. The image was in a sickening shade of green, which Brad explained was night vision on the camera. The green color allowed the human eye to distinguish the images better, as the actual image was in black and white. "Let's fast-forward a bit," he said tapping the cue button. The screen jumped and jittered as he sped through the footage. After a few seconds, there was a flash of light and the image was completely white.

"Shit," he growled.

Angel shook her head and turned.

"What?" I asked, obviously the only one out of the loop.

"You turned on the light," Brad said. "That tends to screw up night vision cameras."

"I turned the light back off," I defended myself.

"May not have helped," Brad said, punching the cue button again. "It takes these older lenses a while to adjust. Prolonged exposure like that can severely damage them."

I ran my fingers nervously over my mouth. "I'm so sorry," I said, turning to Angel. "I didn't even know there was a camera in there."

She waved off my apology.

"Wait," Brad said with a hint of excitement in his voice, "we may have something."

All eyes focused on the display as the solid white image started to fade to black. Slowing down the cue speed, Brad inched forward frame by frame. The blackness was replaced with a green hue as objects became visible in the frame.

I recognized myself sitting on the edge of the bed. "This is it! She should be—"

Before I could finish the thought, a bright green light flashed in front of the camera and disappeared. It happened in a matter of frames. Tilting his head slightly at the sight, he stopped the tape, wound it back and played it at full speed. What took a matter of frames in slow motion happened in a tenth of a second at actual speed. The camera had barely focused on the bed, then the flash, and me standing up and running for the door. Brad repeated the clip several times at varying speeds, but none of us could make out more than what was probably a bright flash in the room at the time.

Brad rubbed his chin. "Did you turn on a light again?"

"No," I answered honestly. "It was completely dark. Could the camera have captured Wednesday walking past it?"

"Wednesday?" Angel echoed.

"My," I paused, "pet name for her."

Angel tried to hide a smile, but I caught a hint of it before it vanished. "Who is this woman?"

I shrugged. "I don't know. She just keeps showing up."

126

Brad, meanwhile, was still busily watching the clip. "Let me dub this over to digital and see if I can clean it up. It could be nothing more than a lens flare, or the camera trying to auto-adjust, but it might be your mystery woman."

"Get on it," Angel instructed and turned back to me. "Jesus, Jack, you look like hell. Try and get some sleep, huh?"

"Thanks," I replied snidely, but that was exactly what I wanted.

"Let Brad work without us hovering over his shoulder," Angel added.

I nodded. "Thank you, both of you."

"No problem, Chief," Brad said with a mock salute. "Get some sleep."

Walking out of the study, I headed straight for the master bedroom. Closing the door behind me, I peeled off my shirt again, but this time I made sure I kept the light off. And slept with one eye open.

It was going to be a long night.

Chapter Fourteen

I didn't feel very rested when I woke up, although that didn't surprise me much. Between watching for black, vaporous apparitions and Wednesday to appear in my bedroom, I hadn't got much sleep. Sitting up, my body popped and ached in protest. I looked down at my chest. Several dark purple bruises had formed on my side where I hurt my ribs, and my fingertips looked as though I had tried to stuff them into a paper shredder. I was a wreck.

There was one saving grace, however: the smell of fresh brewed coffee. Stumbling out of bed, I snatched a clean t-shirt and tried to get my head and limbs into the holes. Finally deciding it was good enough as I reached the door, I sauntered almost drunkenly into the hallway following the rich aroma. Snatching someone's lighter and pack of cigarettes from the kitchen counter—I had no idea who they belonged to, nor did I really care at that point—I drew one of the coffin nails and lit it with the stolen lighter. Tasting the smoke, I pulled it away and smacked my lips. It was terrible. I took another drag to confirm my findings. Yep, utterly terrible. Placing the cigarette back in my mouth, I turned toward the coffee.

"Morning, Jack," Angel said, leaning against the counter with a steaming mug cradled in her hands. Damn, she was blocking the coffee pot. "You're welcome for the cigarette."

I think I grumbled a response, but wasn't

certain it was even English. My brain hadn't activated yet. I looked down at the smoldering cigarette in my hand then back up to Angel, registering what she had said. "Thank you."

She nodded. "How did you sleep?"

"Coffee." I coughed with no regard to her question. I think the obvious answer was standing before her.

Stepping out of my way, she watched as I rummaged through empty cabinets looking for something to dispense the coffee in. As my search came up empty, I wondered if I could pour the coffee straight down my throat. Cigarette dangling from my lips, I placed my hands on the counter and sized up the pot. I figured I could do it.

"Here," Angel said finally, I think enjoying my discomfort.

I looked down to see her slide me a tall, black mug. Her name, vocation, and phone number were emblazoned on the side in silver. Sighing in relief, I hurriedly poured a heady shot of the eye opener.

"I got these as a promotional thing a few months ago," she admitted. "Thought it would be good for business."

I didn't care. I lifted the steaming mug to my lips and sipped the coffee. Oh baby…

"Gave out a couple then lost interest. I keep most of them in my trunk." She laughed. "For just such an occasion."

I enjoyed the sensation of the warm beverage sliding down my esophagus and into my stomach. Ah, the ambrosia of the Gods… After four more cups or so, I would almost feel human again.

"So," the paranormal investigator took a long, obnoxious sip of her coffee, "your naked, mystery chica reappear last night?"

I shook my head. Holding the mug tightly in my hand, I cradled it close to my chest feeling like a predatory animal protecting my kill. I took another drag of the cigarette and exhaled the blue-gray cloud of smog with satisfaction.

"No one else saw her," Angel reported. "The house was basically pretty quiet. Jazz said she had a lamp flicker on and off a few times, but that could be bad wiring. We're checking the outlet right now."

"Wow," I breathed, "this is a full service outfit. Got any plumbers on staff? The sink in the master bedroom won't drain right. I think it's haunted."

"I don't appreciate your sarcasm, Jack," Angel scolded. "What my team does is try and find rational, real world explanations for these events. I would much rather tell someone they had bad wiring than an evil spirit was living in their house. Make sense?"

"The simplest explanation is most often correct," I offered. It was my Zen-ism for the day. My brain hurt now. I needed more coffee, and no more of these terrible cigarettes. I held out the cheap, stolen cigarette. Eyeing it, I dropped it into the sink and doused it. It was better than it deserved.

Angel smiled as if reading my mind. Either I was an open book, or there was a bad case of ESP going around.

I took another sip of coffee. "What's the plan, el jefe?"

"I hate that word," Angel replied. "It sounds like 'heifer.' Not very attractive, you know?"

I shrugged off her criticism. "So…?"

"This may sound stupid," Angel started, "but my team always gets better results at night. It seems like there's more spirit activity then." She paused, considering her theory. "Most of us have been up all night. We're going to head home, get some rest, and meet back here around three. Sound like a plan?"

"Sure," I said, "it's as good as anything else." I was trying to be macho and nonchalant, but her proposal scared the hell out of me. I didn't want to be left alone in the house.

"I suggest you don't stay here today," Angel offered with a twinkle in her eye.

She was reading my mind! I knew it!

"I am not." She laughed. "I just think you should get out and enjoy some fresh air." She set her mug on the counter and stepped toward me. "This thing," Angel lowered her voice, "whatever it is, really doesn't like you. I don't think you should be here alone."

I felt the house shudder as if it had heard.

Angel and I exchanged worried glances.

"Don't leave until I shower," I said almost pleadingly.

Angel patted my shoulder. "Hurry."

Dropping the mug on the counter with an accidental clunk, I charged back into the master bedroom. Tearing off my clothes en route, I hit the bathroom completely naked. Predominantly white gold fixtures accented the sink and shower/bathtub. Snagging one of the towels I had stolen from the

131

hotel, I slipped it over the gold towel rack and twisted on the shower taps.

I felt a buzz over my skin like static electricity.

As I waited for the water to warm (it was an old house after all) I headed back into my bedroom and hurriedly collected a set of clothes from my suitcase. Keeping a wary eye on The Hollow, I squatted down, flipped open the top of the case and dug my hand in. I felt a sharp pain tear into the back of my hand. Yelping, I ripped it free and crumbled back onto my butt. Cradling my hand, I lifted it to see a streak of maroon. Wiping the blood away with my thumb, I stared at a deep puncture just above my second knuckle. Applying direct pressure, I tried to stop the flow of blood.

Rolling onto my knees, I peered carefully into the suitcase as if I expected something to jump out and bite me—which, truthfully, wouldn't surprise me at this point. Letting go of my wounded hand, I reached back into the case carefully and began to pull articles of clothes free. As I set each aside, I searched for anything that could have done the damage. There wasn't anything there, nothing that could have caused the cut anyway. Pulling another shirt free, I saw something move.

I yanked my good hand back instantly.

Holding my breath, I stared into the case. Nothing inside it moved.

Using my fingertips, I cautiously reached in and lifted a pair of jeans. Peeking beneath, I couldn't see anything. I stared intently and slowly lifted them higher. Maybe it was just my imagination, or overexhaustion causing me to see

132

things. I'm honestly not prone to hallucinations. Even during my drug phase in high school, I stayed pretty level-headed. As my courage gathered, I wrapped my hand around the jeans and yanked them free. I spotted what looked like a hairy, dark splotch in the corner of the case. I leaned closer out of curiosity.

Dumb, Jack, real dumb.

The hairy, black splotch reared up, hissed like a snake, and shot out directly at me. Rolling onto my butt again, I watched the splotch sail past my head and land on the floor behind me with a thump. Spinning with a squeak of my naked flesh, my eyes snapped down. Forgetting to breathe, I was almost instantly on my feet. The splotch turned out to be a massive tarantula.

I glanced worriedly down at the cut on my hand. Had I been bitten? Not really a spider expert, despite being a horror author, I had no idea what a bite looked like, or what the tarantula's venom did to flesh. Had I been envenomed?

My eyes locked on the spider. It was, as far as I could tell, watching me too. As I moved, so did it. Its oversized pipe cleaner legs worked carefully and systematically, keeping it perfectly aimed at me. It meant to strike again. It was merely sizing me up.

What I wouldn't give for a can of Raid.

The tarantula leapt.

I threw my arm out and tried to bat the arachnid out of the air, but its reflexes were faster than mine. The spider's legs snapped around my wrist like cuffs, and this time I felt it bite.

I grunted and shook my arm violently as pain

radiated up it. I felt the spider slip free and heard it hit the floor. Stumbling back, still cradling my bloody hand, I searched for the spider but there was no sight of it. Pain throbbed angrily up my arm, and my flesh around the bite felt like it was on fire. Moving to an open area, while avoiding the stupid bearskin rug, I nervously scanned the floor. I wanted to turn and run for the door, but I knew if I turned my back the tarantula would be on me again. I gritted my teeth as my vision blurred. The venom was working quickly.

I had to get out of here. No choice.

Backing up to the door, I wrapped my bloody hand around the knob. I was about to run out of my bedroom completely naked, but by this point, I didn't really care. It was either this, I stared down at the bite marks on my arm which had already turned midnight black, or die. Out of the corner of my eye, I saw movement again. My head snapped toward it and I spotted the tarantula skittering along the far baseboard. It was coming straight for me, much faster than I thought a spider its size could move. It was going to attack. If I turned now, I was toast.

I had to time this right.

Twisting the knob, I heard the bolt disengage. Trying to ignore the pounding in my head, I watched the massive arachnid speed closer. Its legs made a sickening click as they hit the hard wood. I took a single step to my left, and the spider adjusted its attack vector accordingly. It was almost on me. It was now or never.

The spider leapt.

I moved.

134

Pulling open the door, I threw it hard out and heard the arachnid hit with a crunch. Sliding into the hallway, I fell back against the wall and froze. Waiting for any movement, I stared at the open door. I think I got it.

I threw my head back and laughed, "How do you like that, you son of a bitch? Squished your hairy ass!"

I heard a snicker from my right.

Turning my head slowly, I saw Jazz, Singe, and Jared watching me with amusement from the end of the hall.

Turning, I started to protest, but realized something: I didn't hurt anymore. I lifted my hand but didn't see a trace of the cut or any blood. Looking over my opposite arm, the bite mark had completely vanished. It had all been in my head. The Hollow was messing with me. I turned back to the threesome. "I think I'm gonna hit the shower."

They nodded, unwilling to turn. Singe giggled, but tried to stifle it with the back of her hand.

"All right then," I said, snapping my fingers nervously, "shower time." I felt utterly stupid, but not without vindication.

I walked back into the master bedroom and anxiously peered behind the door. There was, as I expected, no trace of the spider.

I had to get out of the house.

Rushing into the steam-filled bathroom, I jumped in the shower and scrubbed as quickly as I could. Even when I lathered shampoo into my hair and the suds ran down my face, I kept my eyes wide open.

135

Chapter Fifteen

It was an utterly cold and miserable day in Union. Not wanting to go all the way in to New York, I had instead opted to wander the town aimlessly. Unfortunately, my decision had been made prior to leaving The Hollow and before my encounter with the spooky spider, so I was unsurprisingly ill equipped for the weather. As I walked headlong into the bone-chilling wind and sleet, I had already developed a lovely sniffle. It was turning out to be one helluva a day.

Hiking up my collar high on my neck, I succeeded more in trapping the wind than deflecting it. I pulled my hands up into my sleeves and stuffed them deep into my pockets to create some warmth. I had heard that it rained vertically in New York, and as icy raindrops repeatedly smacked into my face, I was starting to believe it. I think my teeth were chattering so loudly that others unlucky enough to be caught in the storm could hear them.

I spotted an elderly homeless man sitting against the wall of a store, his knees pulled tightly to his chest. He was old and haggard, and his clothes were tattered and threatening to fall off at any moment. A worn stocking hat was pulled low on his head, doing its best to cover the man's ears. His scruffy face was red and battered, while his eyes seemed little more than hardened slits staring out of his skull.

That was my future.

All obsessions either make or break you, and

most often, they break you. You give everything in their pursuit or acquisition, but usually come up short or wanting. That was the way of obsessions: once is never enough.

I hadn't really considered it much, but running through the night chasing after ghosts had cost me a lot already. I hadn't written a complete novel in over a year (the manuscript James trashed was completed before Irene's death). I had lost contact with most of my friends simply because I didn't have the desire to deal with them, and even my agent had grown weary of waiting on me and stopped returning most of my calls. I was nearly fifty pounds lighter than this time last year because eating was another hassle I simply didn't have time for and my smoking and drinking vices had grown to monumental levels. I was a wreck, though I would never admit that out loud.

And what was I doing this all for? My dead wife who didn't even want me? She had only come home after her lover had found someone else to dip his wick in. Irene left me…left the home, comfort, and lifestyle I provided her. Why? Because she was bored. I knew that was oversimplifying the answer, but I felt it was the truth. Why was I searching her out now? Was it for her salvation, or my own? Did I really want to apologize to her, and give her some kind of peace in the afterlife, or did I want her to apologize to me? Maybe I just wanted to hear her say she loved me one last time. I wasn't exactly sure what I wanted.

"It is awake."

I stopped and looked down at the old bum. "I'm

sorry, did you say something?"

The bum didn't answer and made no movement to acknowledge my question, or even my presence. I stared at him for a long time, finally seeing him blink. I let out a long breath and watched it disappear before me. Turning away, I started back on my way.

A hand snapped up and clamped hard around my wrist.

I spun to find the old bum holding me, his eyes as black as coal. They were horrible and inhuman, but somehow very familiar. Though the exterior was different, I knew for certain I had gazed upon this soul before. It sent a shudder straight to my core.

"It is awake," the old bum wheezed, "and it wants you."

I shook my arm hard trying to break free. The old bum refused to break his grip and continued to stare at me. His mouth contorted into a toothy grin showing his terrible yellow and black teeth. Horror gripped me, and forced me to act. Kicking up hard, the old bum's head snapped back with a crack. Falling back, his fingers loosened enabling me to rip free of his grasp. The bum coughed and sputtered then fell to the cold, wet sidewalk in a heap.

I did the only thing I could think of: I ran. Ducking into a nearby store, I stopped short after spotting my own face.

Crap.

I had unfortunately chosen a bookstore, and even more unfortunately, this one was featuring my latest novel. A tall stand-up display with at least twenty copies of Jessie's Warning, and my oh-so-trying-to-be-mysterious mug, stood waiting in front of the cash register. The big yellow lettering at the top, attributed to someone, who was no doubt in the publisher's pocket, from Newsweek, proclaimed "Jessie's Warning...is Devlin's best work since Five 'Till Midnight." I knew it was true, but it was still a slap in the face. What about the twelve books published between?

Ah, screw 'em.

The likelihood of an author, even a best seller such as myself, getting recognized on the street was slim. Most of us just didn't have the public profile that celebrities had, unless you count Stephen King, and he's just weird enough to stick in your mind. I mean, who doesn't remember him from Creepshow covered in green fuzz after touching the meteor, then blowing his head off with a shotgun? Now that was great! Still, I pulled my collar over my face and nose and ducked into one of the aisles, doing my best Snidely Whiplash impression. Twirling my imaginary mustache, I snickered devilishly and went about my work tying the damsel in distress to the railroad tracks.

The bookstore, small compared to some of the others I had attended signings at, was cozy and most importantly, warm. Shaking off some of the cold that had accumulated on me, I walked slowly down the aisle I had stumbled into and perused the covers. Graceful images of beautiful women and incredibly chiseled men stared out from the romance section. With idiotic titles like Gabrielle's Rendezvous, Private Passionate Pleasures, and Warm Exotic

Embrace, the books sounded more like soft-core porn than romance. I had often secretly wondered if I should write a romance novel under a trashy pen name, but the idea never advanced beyond that. Perhaps I'm just uncreative, but there's only so many ways you can describe sex. It's basically insert tab A into slot B, rinse and repeat.

Shaking my head, I browsed the store's selection. Maybe this was just what I needed. I could find a paperback then head over to that little coffee shop I found two nights ago. That was exactly what I needed today. Good. At least I had a plan. Now to find a book... I stared at the bold face names on the covers and tried to find one I didn't recognize. The one universal truth I had learned early in the publishing industry is that most other authors are assholes. I don't like to comment on their writing skills, but as people, they generally suck. That's just my two cents though, and yes, I can make change.

"Aren't you Jack Devlin the author?"

Without turning toward the voice, I felt my heart sink. Remember what I said about being recognized? Apparently I was wrong. I had two options at this point. I could 'fess up, sign a book and be on my way, or feign ignorance and try and weasel out (see what I mean about authors being assholes?). Neither option was overly appealing, as I just wanted to be left alone, but I was going to have to bite the bullet.

I turned and stopped. "You little bitch."

"Is that any way to greet an old friend?" Wednesday chided me as she threw her arms around me. "Nice to see you again, Jack!" She hugged me tightly, then pulled away. "See how that works? Now you try." She opened her arms and closed her eyes.

I stepped around her and walked away.

"You are not a people person, are you, Jack?" I heard Wednesday call from behind me.

"Leave me alone," I growled, "or I am going to buy a gun and shoot you in the face."

"Violent too." She laughed. Her black hair was pulled up on top of her head again, only two strands of purple fell down over her eyes. "New York has the seven day waiting period on all firearm sales for mandatory background checks." She shrugged. "Sorry, Jack."

"Look," I lowered my voice and stepped close to the marionette, "if you don't leave me alone, I will kick your ass. I don't care if you're a woman or not."

"Then I will have the vast Devlin fortune." Wednesday smiled. "Because I will sue your ass so fast it'll make your head spin."

She had me there. I stepped back. "What do you want, Wednesday?"

"I keep telling you..." She reached out for my arm, but I stepped away. Ignoring the brush off, she continued, "I'm here to help."

"Help?" I threw my arms into the air. "Help with what? The black shapeless thing that likes to throw me down the stairs? Or maybe with Satan, who's stomping mad and apparently lives in my attic, or how about this odd little goth girl who keeps showing up in the strangest places? What can

141

you help me with, Wednesday?"

Wednesday shook her head condescendingly. "Wow, you need a serious attitude adjustment, mister."

That was it. I was going to kill her.

"Can I help you two?"

I turned to see a thin, elderly woman with a white nametag pinned to her sweater looking nervously at the two of us.

"Yes, do you have the latest Jack Devlin novel?" Wednesday asked sweetly.

I glared at the evil goth girl.

"Yes we do," the elderly clerk replied. She started back toward the counter, all the while keeping a wary eye on us.

I wasn't sure if she was going to help us, or call the cops.

She stopped next to the display and snatched a copy of Jessie's Warning. "Here's Devlin's latest."

"Have you read it?" Wednesday asked without missing a beat.

"No." The elderly clerk smiled. "I'm more of a Jackie Collins fan." She looked very much like an elderly June Cleaver from Leave It To Beaver, complete with white sweater and pearls strung around her neck.

Wednesday laughed. "You know, so am I, but my guy here loves Jack Devlin. I'm not sure why."

I tried not to delve into how surreal this situation had become. I looked at clerk June, smiled and shrugged.

Wednesday held the novel to her chest lovingly, then turned back to me. "If I buy this, will you autograph it for me?"

Crap.

June's eyes widened. She looked at the cardboard display then back to me, visually confirming who I was. "You're Jack Devlin!"

I was going to kill Wednesday. I sighed and nodded. "Yes."

Rushing around the counter, June picked up her cell phone and began to dial a number. "I have to get Amy, the owner, in here. She's one of your biggest fans!"

I froze. The name rang a bell. "Thin, blonde, and wears a fuzzy, pink coat?"

Clerk June nodded. "That's her."

I remembered the creepy, Kathy Bates like woman from the diner, and the offer to let me study her. "We've met." I'd rather be at The Hollow at this point.

"My," Wednesday said with mock surprise, "you do get around, don't you?"

I listened to June explain that I was in the store, and how creepy Kathy Bates like Amy should get down here as quickly as possible. Neat. Stepping up to Wednesday while clerk June was distracted, I angrily grabbed the goth girl's arm and spun her toward me. "What the hell do you think you're doing?" I asked her while jabbing my finger into her chest.

"Well I was going to have you autograph this novel, but now I don't think I like you anymore." Wednesday ripped her arm free and set the novel on a nearby shelf. "I keep offering to help you, and doing nice things for you, and what do I get in

143

return?"

I waited for the obvious answer.

"Bullshit," she answered without hesitation. "That's all you give me, Jack. Fine." She pushed angrily past me and marched toward the door. "That's it. I've had enough. You're on your own."

"Fine," I echoed.

She scowled. "I hope you remember this as you lay dying inside The Hollow. I hope my face is the last fucking thing you see, Jack. Throwing you off the stairs and the spider? Those were just starters."

She blew through the door, the bell above jingling so loudly that I thought it was about to break from its mount.

I watched Wednesday stride away from the store into the ever worsening storm. I was so angry, it barely registered she wasn't wearing anything that would keep her warm, let alone a coat. She turned a corner and vanished out of my sight. Maybe she would freeze to death and I would find a Wednesdaycicle. At least that brought a smile to my face.

"Mr. Devlin?"

I turned back to clerk June hoping she was going to offer me cookies.

She folded her hands neatly. "Do you mind waiting a few minutes?"

I thought of Wednesday walking away. I couldn't think of anything else. "Why?"

"Amy says she needs to get cleaned up before she comes down," June explained.

Oh lord. Amy thought I had come to collect on her offer to "study." I rolled my head around my tired neck then ran my hand up and massaged it hard with my fingers. For some strange reason, I couldn't explain why, stress was gathering at the base of my skull. And yes, I was being sarcastic. "I really don't have time," I said apologetically. "I just stopped in for a book. I actually have plans."

"Oh?" clerk June said in that motherly way that placates, yet knows you are lying. "That's too bad. Amy will be ever so disappointed."

"I'm sorry." Not that I wanted to disappoint Amy or anything, but my dance with the spider this morning had made me cranky. Something flickered in my mind. "Wait..."

Clerk June cocked her eyebrow obviously confused (I had that effect on people). "Wait? For what?"

"She said spider," I thought aloud. Dropping my head, I ran my fingers into my hair and shook gently hoping to somehow activate my brain. I grunted as I felt the hamster wheel slowly start to spin. "How did she know about the spider?" I posed the question to June as if she would have an answer. I shook my head. "She wasn't there."

I stopped in mid-thought and spun to face the door. There wasn't any use in charging after her as she had a nasty knack for disappearing into thin air. She was already gone.

June looked even more confused, and a little concerned about my mental state. "What are you talking about, exactly?"

"Think," I instructed myself. "How would she know?"

I turned away from June without another word

and shot toward the exit. I heard June shout behind me, but her protests were silenced by the closing door.

The storm hit me like a brick wall. Lowering my head, I plowed into it. The massive, cold raindrops hit my face hard. Pushing around the corner, I scanned for Wednesday. To my dismay, she was gone. The sidewalk before me was empty, and there was only a smattering of traffic on the road.

How the hell did she know about the spider? There was only one logical answer: she was there... Somehow, some way, she was spying on me. She seemed to have free run of my home, so it wasn't beyond reason that she had installed cameras. But what, ultimately, was her angle? That was the piece of the puzzle I was missing. What did she want? My blood ran cold as I came to the only, inescapable answer:

Me.

Chapter Sixteen

I sat alone on The Hollow's front porch, my leather jacket wrapped tightly around me, though I wasn't shivering. The rain had gradually turned into huge, magnificent flakes that floated gently to the ground, and somehow, I couldn't explain why, it felt warmer now. My mother always claimed it was warmer when it snowed, but I thought she was full of it. How could it be warmer? Water was freezing in midair! Logic aside, it seemed, for the moment anyway, Mom was right. I looked up into the swirling snow and became transfixed. My mind began to wander.

Irene.

Of course it would instantly wander to her. I was swept into the vastness of my memory, a dark ocean of thoughts of her and myself, and I could see myself in the center moving further and further into deepening waters. Completely naked, I had only what I carried inside to protect me from the ebb and flow. But was I drowning or waving?

Whoa, got a little purple there for a moment.

My head hurt, but it wasn't pounding. It felt like there was a build-up of pressure directly behind my forehead and eyes. Most would write it off to allergies, but I didn't have any I was aware of. I was exhausted, both physically and mentally. This quest, this obsession, had taken everything I had, and so far returned nothing. And why was I chasing ghosts? It was a question I kept coming back to, but never had a satisfactory answer for. Maybe I had simply gone out of my mind.

It wasn't that far of a trip, anyway.

I felt the breast pocket of my coat vibrate, followed by the annoying chirp of my cell phone. Digging it out of my pocket, along with another cigarette from the pack I had picked up at a gas station down the street, I flipped open the clamshell and stared at the name and number displayed. I sighed and slipped the cigarette between my lips. It was James, or more likely, Janice calling for him. My thumb hovered over the send button. Probably they had just discovered my manuscript was missing. He was either calling to ask for another copy, or to yell at me for stealing it. I was fairly certain of the latter. But maybe it was Janice calling to tell me James had been fired and I was being assigned a new editor... No, that call would have come from my agent. I didn't want to talk to him. Thumbing the rocker on the left side, I toggled the phone into silent mode and snapped it shut. Slipping it back into my pocket, I lit my cigarette.

I looked up to see Singe saunter up the sidewalk toward me. Her steps slowed as she neared The Hollow. The wind was blowing her blonde hair over exposing more of her punkish black roots. A puffy, purple coat appeared to be slowly devouring her, but at least she looked warm. She spotted me on the porch. "Hi, Mr. Devlin."

"Singe." I flicked an ash and greeted her.

Probably in her mid-twenties, although I wasn't the best judge in that area, I was certain Singe was a geek's wet dream come to life. She had a punk princess vibe to her that was a little offsetting to me—a sure sign I was getting old. Sitting on the porch next to me, her coat opened revealing a baby doll t-shirt with several characters I recognized from Star Wars done in Japanese anime style. "I can't believe it's snowing again. Weatherman said it would be warmer today."

Ah, weather discussion: the last bastion of two souls who had absolutely nothing to say to each other.

"I don't even bother watching the weather anymore," I admitted. "It's too much like playing the lottery." Wow, I wasn't just getting old, I was old.

Singe laughed softly.

I felt my cell phone vibrate in my pocket again, but made no move to answer it. "So," I exhaled cigarette smoke, "how did you hook up with Angel?"

"I found her card." She raked her fingers through her wet, windblown hair trying to make something of it. "Then I called her."

She wasn't much for conversation. I had concluded that within ten minutes of meeting her. She was a listener. It was either talk business, or sit in silence. I chose the first. "Did you have a chance to review my digital recordings last night?"

"Yeah." She nodded.

I waited for the remainder of her report, but when it was apparent it wasn't forthcoming, I had to prod her a bit. "Did you hear anything?" I took the final drag of my smoke then flicked the butt away. "Any of the voices?"

"No." Singe frowned. "The only voice on the

recordings was yours."

"Wait." I felt like I had been sideswiped. "There should have been at least two. I was certain it was still recording when Wednesday showed up. It should have captured her voice." I was getting a really bad feeling about my goth stalker girl.

"I have it here." She dug my digital recorder out of her coat pocket and handed it to me. "I've marked the areas where you claimed to have heard voices so you can skip right to them."

I nodded and lifted the recorder to my ear. Pressing the play button, I cycled to the first bookmark Singe had created. I listened to my voice asking a question, but she was right, there was nothing more. None of the voices or sounds I had heard were captured on the recording. I jumped to the second bookmark and heard my voice carrying on a very one-sided conversation. No trace of Wednesday's voice could be heard. I was completely dumbfounded.

I snapped off the recorder and turned to Singe. "What the hell…?"

She shrugged. "It sounds like you're having a conversation. You pose and answer questions, but there are no other voices that I could discern."

"Have you run it through a computer?" I looked down at the slender, silver device. "Sometimes the internal speakers on these aren't that great."

"I haven't," Singe admitted. "Give me a chance to listen tonight, before the séance."

A chill ran up my back, and it wasn't the weather. "A séance? Are you serious?"

Singe stood up. "Standard procedure," she

answered matter-of-factly. "Angel conducts them during every investigation."

The word conjured up images of a ragged, old, skeletal gypsy with a red bandana covering her graying black hair, seated at a small, round table with a glowing crystal ball before her. I had heard way too many horror stories about séances to take them seriously, and wasn't entirely sure I wanted to take part in one. The idea struck me as more than a little hokey. Still, Angel was legit as far as I could tell, and she was a conduit. "Do they produce results?"

"Always." Singe smiled for the first time. It was small and sweet, with a hint of mischief in the corners, and more than a little sexy. "See you inside, Mr. Devlin," Singe said finally, sounding almost like she was giving me a warning. She turned and walked into The Hollow, shutting the front door quietly behind her.

Standing, I turned and faced The Hollow's front door. I didn't really want to go back in, but I had to. Flashes of giant spiders and murderous black clouds skittered through my thoughts. My ribs ached with every breath I took. Angel told me that whatever was in there was very angry, and wanted me dead. I had no reason not to believe her. Still, I knew more now than ever before, that my answers were inside. I was going to make contact with Irene, or die trying...most likely the latter. Tonight was going to be an interesting night. That much, at least, I knew for sure.

Chapter Seventeen

Feeling like a third wheel, or sixth in this case, I sat quietly in the kitchen sipping coffee as Angel's team checked their equipment and made final preparations for tonight's event. The house was buzzing with activity and communiqués broadcast across squelching radios. Everything, every detail, had to be perfect. Tonight Angel planned to unleash the forces inside The Hollow. And she didn't take that lightly.

I could hear my evil white laptop calling to me from its case in the foyer. It wanted me to retrieve it and attempt to bang out some ideas, but the call was fleeting. I had no current work in progress, or any ideas to develop. My brain was consumed with Irene, The Hollow, and the impending séance. Still, I wondered if I should be keeping some sort of journal. I was a writer after all. I should be writing…something.

Ah, to hell with it. I took another sip of coffee and lit a cigarette.

Looking up, I watched Jared concocting something in a cauldron he had boiling on a portable, electric burner. Ingredients that could almost be a good stew (if you ignored the terrible smell) were scattered about the table in various stages of preparation. A ragged book bound in thick red leather sat open propped against a candle. The pages were old, yellowed, and dog-eared. A few burn marks could be seen on the edges of the pages, showing how much use the book had been put through. Jared paused, ran his finger down the open page then readdressed the cauldron.

I blew a smoke ring out of boredom. "Whatcha making?"

Jared stopped and rubbed his fingers through his red beard. Glancing down, he assessed his ingredients and materials. "Protection talismans for each of us."

"Why?"

"Angel will be unleashing some serious energy tonight." Jared stirred his cauldron. "We have to protect ourselves...just in case."

Jared's tone was calm and even, despite what he was doing and what we all were possibly facing tonight. There were a hundred other places I could have waited in The Hollow, but in the kitchen with this witch seemed the safest. I had the feeling that no matter what came his way, he would take it in stride and let it roll off his back.

"Jack," Jared said my name evenly, "I meant to talk to you about something. Do you have a moment?"

I shrugged and took another drag. "Would seem that way. What's on your mind, Mr. Wizard?"

The witch smirked for a moment as he enjoyed the reference. I was hoping he wasn't too young for it.

Jared put down the wooden spoon he was using to stir the contents in cauldron and gave me his complete and total attention. "I hope you don't mind the intrusion, but I've read your aura."

I wasn't sure how I felt about that statement. Not that it really bothered me, I just don't have a definitive stance on the whole "aura" thing. I can't see it or touch it, so therefore it's hard for me to quantify. I nodded for him to continue.

"One caveat." Jared folded his arms. "Aura reading isn't an exact science. One color or shape might mean something completely different to me than to another person. My interpretation depends heavily on my own experiences." He paused to let me consider his disclaimer. "Is that okay?"

"All right," I said cautiously as if he were about to launch into a sales pitch for volcano insurance. Sure, it seems like a good idea, but when was the last time you had Krakatoa erupt in your front yard? My bullshit shield went up instinctively.

"Your aura is very dark," Jared stated without a hint of judgment in his voice. "The overriding color is gray, with large blobs of black and brown. The gray signifies depression and a dark side to your personality, while the black and brown are intense negativity. Your aura doesn't glow," he said with heavy sadness apparent. "It looks more like smog clinging to you."

I took the last drag of my cigarette then extinguished it in my coffee cup. "Okay," I exhaled the smoke, "so I'm a very negative person."

"No." Jared shook his head. "I've never seen an aura in this condition before. I'm telling you this as a warning. Whatever path you're on," the witch took a breath in through his nose, "is going to cause your destruction."

Well, I already knew that, didn't I?

"It may be too late to alter your fate," Jared added.

154

His statement unsettled me, and the look in his eyes raised goose bumps on my flesh. I had always considered the future as malleable rather than fixed. Yet here was a man in tune with the forces that most of us didn't even come close to understanding telling me that I was doomed. That didn't sit well with me.

I cleared my throat. "Am I going to die?"

"We're all going to die, Jack," Jared reassured me. "It's just a matter of when. You, however," he paused and appeared to be staring at my forehead, "I have no way to gauge. It's hard to see in the darkness. If one stares long enough into the void, the void stares back."

His words were cryptic, creepy, and yet familiar. It was the same thing Angel told me the night we met at the hotel bar.

"Angel hasn't told me why you moved into The Hollow, but I can see just from your aura that your motives aren't just." He shifted uncomfortably. "That makes me wonder if I should even be here at all. The Karmic scale we are all judged by is easily swayed," he warned.

"I—" I started to speak but felt the words die in my throat. His warning was ominous and deadly serious. "I want to see my wife again."

The witch's gaze didn't change. His face remained stern. "This is a precarious path you walk, Jack Devlin. I hope I'm wrong. I hope it doesn't bring you to ruin."

I felt suddenly ashamed. "So you're staying to help me?"

"I'm staying," Jared confirmed, "but not to help

155

you. I'm here for Angel and the other investigators. Whatever it is you're planning," he moved back to his cauldron and began stirring again, "I want no part of it. You are dangerous."

I stared at the witch unsure if I should get up and pop him in the mouth for talking to me that way. Letting my stare fall away, I finally stood from the table and walked slowly out of the kitchen. His words swarmed through my brain like voracious piranha, eating me from the inside out as I walked. The worst part—and I hated myself for even thinking this—was Jared was right. I hadn't ever intended for others to be taken down on my quest, but here I was with six souls on my conscience. I wondered if I should ask Angel and her team to leave, but I knew I needed them…a lot more than they needed me. This was my best shot at contacting Irene, and if The Hollow had a say in the matter, possibly my last.

Stumbling through the foyer, I hit a dead stop. Jazz stood in my path with her hands on her hips. Her stance shouted angry parent.

"Jazz," I greeted her.

"Jack," she replied coolly.

I wasn't sure what to do, or what to say. Had I done something wrong? I felt suddenly as if I were in trouble.

The paranormal investigator smirked. "Do you have a minute?"

"For what?"

Jazz turned and looked at the sun beginning to set out the front windows, "it's almost time for the séance, but there are a few things I think you should

156

know." Without another word, she turned and walked into the octagonal room.

I followed her in, curious now. Maybe she would close the doors, profess her desire for me, and offer to pleasure me in ways most men only dream of. Yeah, that probably wasn't going to happen. Hey, a man can dream, can't he? Jazz sat on the sofa and patted the empty cushion next to her. Ordinarily if a beautiful woman beckoned to me, I would be there in a heartbeat, but Jazz was acting a bit strange. After what Angel had told me about conduits and spirits possessing people to use as instruments, I wasn't entirely sure I felt comfortable being alone in a room with someone I barely knew. Who knew how susceptible Jazz was to the entity's influence? I walked around the room and stood on the opposite side of the coffee table.

Jazz observed me warily for a moment, perhaps sizing me up, or waiting for her moment to strike, maybe even to see if she was in danger. "I did some research on The Hollow this afternoon." She opened a yellow folder on the coffee table. "This place definitely has an interesting history."

Ah, that was her function in the group. I had been trying to figure it out since meeting her. Brad was the video expert, Singe was the audiophile, Jared was the spiritual advisor, and Jazz handled research on a case. Made sense. "What did you find?"

"Some of this you might already know," Jazz prefaced. "The Hollow was built in 1792 by one of the first mayors of Union, Lincoln Ezekiel."

I nodded. "Knew that."

"And he was murdered here in...uh..." She quickly paused and perused her information.

"1799," I finished.

Jazz looked up with a smile. "That's right."

Her smile was stunning. It reminded me of Irene's when... I sighed. It wasn't even worth thinking about. I tried to focus on the here and now. "I was told a little about the house," I admitted. "Why was Ezekiel killed? I was told it was over a land dispute."

"Technically true," Jazz answered, "but that isn't the whole story. Mayor Ezekiel was basically a victim of circumstance. Union was expanding and the town deemed it necessary to have a meeting hall, and it was his signature that authorized it. The hall was built on what was then the south side of town." Jazz flipped a page in her folder. "An Indian tribe, the Cayuga, one of the five original constituents of the Iroquois, claimed that area was sacred land and wanted the hall removed. Ezekiel refused, and was killed right here in The Hollow by several members of the tribe. Apparently they sacrificed him to their gods to appease them, and apologize for the white man treading on sacred space."

"That's bad mojo," I said with detached interest. This all seemed too convenient. Indian burial ground? Hadn't I seen that movie? Well, at least the house wasn't built right on top of it...or was she coming to that part?

"Of course," Jazz flipped another page in her folder, "they never found the alleged Indians responsible. It seems they were blamed for a whole

158

host of problems in Union, but there was never any direct proof." She paused. "From what I found, Mayor Ezekiel wasn't that fantastic of a leader. He pissed off a lot of people. Could have been anyone that whacked him."

I considered the possibility. "Could Ezekiel be haunting The Hollow? No matter who did it, seems like he went out in a bad way."

Jazz sat back on the couch and took a deep breath in through her nose. "It's hard to say. Sometimes I get flashes of personality from entities, little bits of history replayed over and over, but this time..." She let her sentence trail off as her eyes wandered around the octagonal room. "It just feels angry here. With no real rhyme or reason. I don't know."

"Okay." I thought for a moment. "We have one possible suspect. What else did you find?"

"The Hollow's history seems to be very sketchy after Ezekiel's death. It's been set on fire or burned to the ground more times than I can count. The last time was in 1957 and it was almost completely consumed by the blaze."

"The place has had a bit of bad luck," I confirmed.

"A bit? Try over two hundred years of bad luck," Jazz said. "The Hollow is like a bad luck magnet."

Interesting analogy, although somewhat crude. Could a bad luck magnet really exist? And if so, who would want one? I shook my head. I was starting to feel a bit randy. I pulled my cigarette pack out of my pocket and drew one of the slender

159

sticks. Maybe a smoke would calm the shakes…?

"So what about this fire in '57?" I asked, then lit my cigarette. I started to pace. "What happened?"

"Not entirely sure," Jazz admitted. "Newspaper reports claim the cause of the fire could never be determined. A family was killed in the blaze though."

I took another puff. "Who were they?"

Jazz searched through her paperwork, and pulled out a photocopied newspaper article. "The Weylands," she answered. "Family of three. Mom, dad, and daughter all killed in the fire. Daddy Weyland was a career soldier, but that's all I could glean."

"A daughter," I breathed. Seems like there was something there, but I wasn't making the connection. "Seems like an awfully big house for a family of three," I commented.

"Seems like an awfully big house for one eccentric writer," Jazz countered.

"Ah." I smiled. "Touché."

"Seems the Weylands inherited the house from the dad's mother after she died unexpectedly here."

"Every owner of this house dies here," I said, putting two and two together.

"And your name's just been added to the deed," Jazz added, snapping her folder shut.

I didn't really need that last statement from Captain Obvious, but it was the truth. I crossed my arms and took another drag from my cigarette as I considered the facts. Ever since Ezekiel pissed off the Cayuga, every owner of the house met a bad end. Maybe the place was cursed? Did Indians perform curses? It wasn't that a spirit haunted The Hollow, maybe the house itself was doing the haunting?

A killer house? That was a little far-fetched, even by my standards and I had once written a story about a haunted toaster. Still, it seemed to fit the facts.

I tossed my cigarette into the fireplace behind me. "Thanks, Jazz."

She nodded. "Just doing my job. I'm not sure what's going to happen tonight," she bit her bottom lip, "but please be careful. Darkness seems to swirl around you, Jack."

Crap. Now I was getting it from her too. What was this, a conspiracy? I didn't near to hear this from everyone in the house.

I turned away and stared out the window. Whatever was going on in The Hollow, we were about to find out during Angel's séance, and I wasn't sure, but I didn't think we were going to like the answers we got.

On cue, Angel walked in from the dining room. "We're ready to begin."

Chapter Eighteen

We gathered in the dining room shortly after nightfall. The room, which had formerly been unused space, now had a heavy gothic vibe. Angel had personally seen to its decoration, and had spared no expense in the preparations. A large, oval-shaped table sat in the center of the room with comfortable, high-backed office chairs spaced evenly around it. A heavy black tablecloth covered everything and spilled down in heaps onto the floor. Where I was certain the spooky crystal ball should be sitting was instead a tall candelabra, black candles reaching up from its curving, spindly arms. Yellow flames flickered and danced, casting odd shadows across the room. Plants decorated the table, floor, and several newly added end tables that sat against the walls. Their bright green leaves were a stark contrast to the deep brown and black hues of the room. At each place there sat a small bag with a long black cord winding off it. They smelled utterly foul, and I was certain these were the protection talismans Jared had been hard at work on.

Yet there was one further addition that raised the hairs on the back of my neck. Bolted to the wall behind the head of the table was a pair of heavy iron shackles. Unsure of their purpose, I tried to ignore the discomfort that had settled in my stomach.

I turned my attention to the others. Jared, still in his black and white Chucks and heavy robe, walked systematically around the table mumbling in what I assumed was Latin, and wafting smoke from burning sage. Angel told me he was purifying the space so we could begin. Meanwhile, Brad, Jazz, and Singe set up strategic bits of audio and video equipment to capture the séance and anything that might happen. While I sat in the corner of the room smoking, Angel stood next to me, a general coolly assessing the battlefield. Yet there was an awkward stiffness in her stance I hadn't seen before. She was nervous, and rightly so.

I looked back at the shackles, and started to realize what they were used for. My gaze settled back on Angel, and I understood.

"Stop staring at me, Jack," Angel said, then laughed. "You're creeping me out."

"Sorry," I said, averting my eyes.

Angel paused and sized me up. "What's the matter?"

"The séance has left me a bit..." I paused and thumbed through the thesaurus in my mind before reaching the entry I was looking for. "Unsettled. I'm not sure I'm comfortable with the idea."

"Why?" Angel asked.

"Because the house, or whatever the hell is here, already wants to kill me," I explained. "I'm not so sure it's a good idea to summon it and risk pissing it off further."

"A valid point," Angel acquiesced, "but you don't have to worry. My team will ensure your safety."

I turned and watched Jared waving his smoking chunk of sage about the room and almost started laughing. This was her idea of protection? I was so screwed. The sudden urge gripped me to make sure my will was up to date. Ah, to hell with it. I didn't have any relatives left I liked anyway.

Angel laughed to herself as though reading my thoughts again.

I slapped my palm to my forehead as if that would provide a block against her. "Will you stay out of my head?"

"Sorry." She smirked.

"Jack?"

I looked up at Jazz and found myself lost for a moment. I struggled to the surface and drew a forced breath. "Jazz."

She smiled, probably cognizant of what my facial expression meant. Certainly she had seen it before. "Where will you be sitting?"

I turned to Angel.

"To my right," she instructed.

Jazz nodded and returned to her preparations.

I thought about the answer for a moment, but drew a blank. "Why's that important?"

"Power flows right to left in a séance," Angel answered without looking at me. "I'm the conduit, but you're the key."

It sounded like she was making it up on the spot, or I was really grumpy today. I shrugged. Her answer was as good as any other. At least she had some authority in her voice when replying, as if she actually knew what she was doing. I turned away.

I watched one of the newly added plants lift off the table, seemingly unnoticed by everyone else, and settle harmlessly on the floor. That was a little odd. Well, at least it didn't break—

The pot exploded sending chunks of dirt and

plant in all directions.

The loud bang startled everyone causing someone to yelp. It sounded feminine, but looked as though it emanated from Jared as he stood against the wall, his free hand trying to calm his heart through his chest. Some big, bad witch we had protecting us.

I found that I had moved protectively in front of Angel, my arms back around her waist. Letting my hands slip free, I turned and smiled sheepishly at the paranormal investigator. She smiled as if to say, It's okay. Don't worry about it. With a thankful nod, I turned back and walked to the source of the explosion. A heap of black dirt and shards of orange pot were all that remained of the decoration. It looked as though someone had stuffed a quarter stick of dynamite in the bottom of the pot, lit the fuse, and run away laughing.

Great.

Not only was my ghost pissed off and trying to kill me, it had the warped sense of humor of a thirteen year old. This was just getting better and better.

"What the hell was that?" Singe yanked off her black headphones and ran around the table. "Did a bomb just go off?"

"Yeah, the Taliban has targeted my house," I answered snidely.

"Did someone knock that plant off the table?" Jazz asked.

"No." I shook my head. "It floated off, landed on the floor, then exploded."

Jazz' eyes widened. "Seriously?"

I held up two fingers. "Scout's honor."

Angel focused on her video expert. "Did you get it on tape, Brad?"

"Checking now," Brad answered hunkered over a small, handheld video camera.

"I'll clean it up." I started toward the kitchen where the broom and dustpan were kept.

"Wait, Jack," I heard Angel call before I hit the door.

I spun and waited.

"You and I need to meditate before the séance," she said. "Leave that to one of my team."

"Meditate?" I asked much like a child being forced to eat their broccoli. "Why?"

"Our energies need to be in tune for the séance," Angel explained. "We can only do that through meditation. I may be able to connect to the spirit, but your presence is the key to get it here. I need to make sure I can protect you and channel your energy efficiently."

"You really take this crap seriously, don't you?" Sarcasm was my defense mechanism. Some took it better than others.

Angel flicked her hand out quicker than I could react and smacked me upside the back of the head. "Shut up, Jack. Let's go."

It was a very motherly action, but it still pissed me off. Trying to hide the geyser of anger that had erupted in my brain, I set my jaw and clenched my fists. I didn't have anything nice to say, so I kept quiet. I didn't think her taking control of this investigation gave her rights over me too, but here we were. The thought only made me angrier.

Chapter Nineteen

Angel led me into the master bedroom, kicked off her shoes, threw the covers up, and sat Indian style on the bed. Laying her hands palm up on her knees, she motioned with her eyes for me to do the same. Sitting on the edge of the bed, I pulled off my shoes, spun and sat facing her. Crossing my legs, I tried to emulate her as best I could. Her spine seemed very straight, but it hurt when I tried it. My bruised ribs didn't seem to want to cooperate. She leaned her head forward and rolled it to relax her neck. Shaking her hands like a magician about to perform a trick, she resumed her position.

"Okay, Jack," she said slowly, "you need to relax for this to work. I need you to open yourself up."

I was still a bit angry about the smack to the head she'd given me, and I wasn't sure I wanted to relax. Maybe I should smack her back to even the score...?

"I need you to let down your walls," she instructed me.

This was getting a bit too new age for me. I expected to start hearing Yanni or Enya at any moment. "All right, how do I do that?"

Her Hispanic eyes settled unblinkingly on me. "First, you need to trust me."

"I do—"

"No you don't," Angel cut me off. "Don't feed me that bullshit, Jack. You think I'm a charlatan."

I wanted to argue, but she was right. I sighed.

"I'm here to help," she declared. "No matter what you think of my methods, know they get results." She placed her hand on mine in a very comforting fashion. "You have to trust me."

She was right. No matter what I thought about this séance, this could be my best chance to achieve my goals. She wanted to channel the spirit in the house, but I wanted to talk to Irene. This was it. I took a deep breath and nodded at her. "All right. I'm in."

"Good," she said, trying to sound convincing, obviously reading my mind again. "Let's begin. I want you to close your eyes and relax, Jack."

I took a deep breath and slowly exhaled.

"Now, imagine a circle surrounding us completely," Angel instructed me. "The circle is unbroken. It doesn't have to be on the bed or floor, it can be floating in the air around us. Are you imagining the circle?"

I nodded. In my mind's eye, I saw a chalk-white circle that looked very much like an oversized hula-hoop surrounding us. It hovered in the air, just above my waist.

"All right," Angel exhaled. "We need to close the circle. This will grant us protection while we meditate."

My brow furrowed, but my eyes remained closed. "Why do we need to be protected?"

"No talking," Angel snapped without answering my question. "I want you to imagine now that you have a hole in the center of your forehead. This hole will allow access to your mind chakra, or your third eye."

168

I imagined an eyelid forming in my forehead complete with eyelashes and tear duct.

"Good," she said with satisfaction. "Now, in a moment I'm going to ask you to open the hole you've created. When you do so, I want you to imagine energy flowing out from the hole and imbuing the circle we've created. I want you to actually feel it, Jack. Do you understand?"

I was starting to get a little worried, but I did. This seemed a bit beyond Meditation 101 for beginners.

"Okay." She took another breath. "Do it now."

I held my eyes shut tightly and saw the third eye open on my forehead. Immediately my body felt light, and my head throbbed with pressure, as though I had a severe sinus headache. The sudden urge to wretch gripped me, but I fought it back. As the gaping, emotionless eye stared out of my head, I channeled energy toward the circle. I physically felt it move from my body to the circle like strands of thick yarn being slowly pulled through my flesh, and as the energy was transferred, the throbbing in my head began to recede. I felt the hairs on my arms and head tingle as though the air around us had somehow become charged with static electricity. In my mind, I saw the circle expand into a transparent bubble that snapped closed around us with an audible pop. The circle was perfectly spherical, and completely intact, despite traveling through the mattress and sheets below us.

"Very good, Jack," Angel said. Her voice sounded muffled even though she was less than a foot from me.

I opened my eyes to find that nothing had changed. I wasn't certain what I expected, but there was no visible sign of the bubble, if it ever existed outside my mind. Angel was sitting still, her chest rising and falling slowly with her breathing. I felt a sudden disappointment, but wasn't entirely sure why. It was as if I had been expecting a Christmas present—a new, shiny, red bike—and woke up to find nothing under the tree.

"We are now protected from any negative energy or entities," Angel said, her voice still somewhat muffled as though she had a towel over her mouth. "I'm going to attempt to align our energies. This is very important for the séance to work."

I nodded, but didn't say anything. This whole thing had gone from odd to downright kooky.

She reached and took my hand. I felt a ripple of energy flow up my arm then snap back like a wave on the shore.

I ripped my hand away in shock. "What the hell was that?"

"Our energies clashed against each other," Angel answered matter-of-factly, as if it were no big deal.

She tried to take my hand again, but I pulled it from her reach. "You need to explain what the fuck is going on before you do something like that."

She sighed. "I'm sorry." Angel held her hand palm up to me and waited. "We need to synchronize our energies. I'm the conduit, but you're the key. We need to be in harmony."

"Now you're sounding like one of those fluff

170

bunny Wicca users," I accused.

She ignored my insult and offered her hand again.

I stared at her open hand and marveled at her brown flesh for a moment. If I was going to do this, I had to get past my personal prejudices.

I took Angel's hand and immediately felt the snap of energy up my arm again, but this time I was ready. It felt as though my skin was reverberating at a different frequency than hers, and both were vying for dominance. The paranormal investigator offered me her other hand. Taking it into mine, I felt the vibrations intensify. It spread up my arms, pooled in my shoulders, and exploded into my chest. Like sitting atop the washing machine during the spin cycle, our bodies started to shake. Then after a moment—it could only have been a second or two—the rhythm started to change. I felt her energy wash into my arms, splash against my biceps, and then recede back. The cycle repeated and slowed, again and again until it practically vanished leaving me with only the slightest buzz in my skin. My eyes locked with Angel's and I understood we had achieved harmony. In that moment, I felt utterly and completely connected to another living soul in a way I had never experienced before.

It was amazing.

I didn't even notice the darkness coalescing around us.

There was a loud crash and a burst of light above our heads. My hands fell away in surprise and I snapped my head up to the source. Above the imaginary bubble, a great shadow loomed like

171

storm clouds. Vapors, like tentacles, reached out and clawed against the protective barrier causing blue energy to crackle over the spherical surface. In the midst of the cloud, I thought I saw a face, mouth agape as though locked in a horrific roar of rage.

I wanted to flatten myself against the bed, to get as far away from the darkness as I could. "What the hell is that?"

"Don't move," Angel warned me and tried to grab my hands again.

Fear propelled me away from the dark mass as it struck the sphere again and again. "Screw this!"

Angel lunged forward with a strength and speed I wasn't aware she possessed. Throwing me to the bed like a professional wrestler, she pinned my arms down and held me in place. "Don't move," she barked. "If you break the boundary, it will cause the sphere to collapse!"

I fought her. I didn't care. I wanted out of here. Right. Now.

"Jack! Stop it!" Angel threw all of her considerable weight on me and struggled against me. "It will get in!"

That stopped me.

It hadn't occurred to me that I could be damning myself by trying to flee. My eyes locked on the black entity. Its face contorted with rage as it clawed against the barrier. I couldn't breathe. Unsure if it was the phantom or the overweight Hispanic woman on top of me, I struggled to draw breath.

"Get off," I whispered hoarsely.

With my wrists pinned beneath her hands,

Angel drew up onto her knees placing us in a very intimate position. Her dark hair fell down around our heads and brushed my face. Like a free diver breaking the surface of the water, I sucked in filling my lungs with precious oxygen. Slowly, I regained my composure and my eyes settled on Angel's face. The intimate connection I had felt only moments before returned and I felt at peace again.

"Jack?" Angel whispered in a husky bedroom voice. "Are you okay?"

Exhaling, I nodded. I looked past Angel. The entity was gone. I returned my gaze to the paranormal investigator on top of me. "It's gone."

She nodded. "I know."

I waited.

"You can get off," I suggested.

She nodded again. "I know."

I had the urge to twist my hips and buck her off, but I didn't think I would be able to accomplish my goal. "Please get off."

Angel smiled. "You're no fun." Letting go of my wrists, she sat straight up and then dismounted off me.

Rubbing my wrists, I sat up. "Where did it go?"

"I don't know," Angel answered. "The protective barrier drew it out, but it vanished when it couldn't penetrate the circle."

I eyed her warily. "Did you know that was going to happen?"

"Once we step off the bed, the barrier will be broken," she said instead. "We should probably get back to the others and start the séance while our energies are in sync."

I snapped my hand around her arm and stopped Angel before she could step off the bed. "Did you know that was going to happen?" I asked again.

Her eyes fell away from me.

"You did," I said. "You were using me. You were using me as bait!"

"No," Angel said quickly.

I let go of her arm. "Why did you do it?"

"I told you the truth," she said defensively. "We did need to align our energies."

"But we didn't need a protective barrier to do it," I spat back. "You wanted to provoke the entity and draw it out. And you knew that little bubble of yours would piss it off." I paused. "But why?"

She turned away from me.

"Why did you do it, Angel?"

Angel remained silent.

"Please," I begged.

She turned and looked at me with sullen eyes. "I needed to test the entity's strength. I had to assess the danger level for the séance."

I let my head fall back with a sigh. "So I was the worm on a big fucking hook. Nice."

"I'm sorry, Jack." Angel frowned. "I didn't…"

"Save it." Stepping off the bed, I felt the static charge in the air dissipate as the circle was broken. I scanned the room for the phantom, but found no trace of it. Turning, I started for the door. "I assume you still have to prepare for the séance?" I asked without looking back.

"I do," Angel replied quietly.

Opening the door, I stepped aside. "Then you best get to it."

That was all that needed to be said. My feelings on the matter were very clear. Head hung low and tail tucked firmly between her legs, Angel walked out of the room like a scolded dog. Watching her go, I reached up and pinched the bridge of my nose hoping my anger would abate. With a sigh, I grabbed the door handle and started to turn.

"Oh, Jack…"

The elongated vowel of my name sent a shiver straight down my spine as though I had just taken too big a bite of ice cream. I knew that voice. I wasn't going to turn. There was no way—no humanly way—she could be in here. There had been absolutely no one in the room with Angel and I. I didn't want to turn. I sighed again. I was really starting to hate this house. And her.

I turned and found her just as I knew I would.

"Jack," she cooed. "We have to talk, Sweetie."

I snapped. Without a moment's hesitation, I spun and grabbed her.

Stomping angrily down the hallway, I headed straight for the dining room. My hand was clamped like a handcuff around her wrist, dragging her literally kicking and screaming. She latched onto the kitchen's doorframe with her free hand, but I angrily ripped her free. Spinning her in front of me, I bent down and slung her over my shoulder like a sack of potatoes. A little heavier than she looked, my knees started to buckle, but I clamped my arm over the evil marionette's back and continued on. I would not be made a fool of again. This time I had her.

"What the fuck are you doing, Jack?"

Gritting my teeth, I made it to the foyer. I grunted as she dug her nails into the soft flesh of my lower back.

"Put me down!"

"Shut up, Wednesday," I growled. I could see the dining room on the opposite side of the octagonal family room. "You're not pulling a Houdini on me again."

Wednesday screamed and pounded her fists on my spine. She must have hit a nerve because my legs were suddenly made of gelatin. I quivered and felt as though we were both heading to the floor. Somehow I fought through it and regained my strength. She writhed and squirmed on my shoulder like an angry cat fighting for freedom but I buckled down and would not let go. I was mere feet from the dining room and could hear the bustle of activity inside.

I was almost there.

Charging through the family room, I then skidded to a stop just inside the dining room. Everyone was there, including Angel, who seemed to be overseeing the preparations with a scowl and dark storm cloud hanging over her head.

I shouted for their attention and slipped Wednesday off my shoulder. "This," I said with my hands clamped on the marionette's upper arms, "is Wednesday."

Angel and her team paused, unsure of what to say or do.

Wednesday lifted her hand and waved. "Hi."

"The girl who has been stalking me and broke into The Hollow," I reiterated.

There was a simultaneous, "Oh," from the crowd.

I almost wanted to slap my forehead in frustration. "I found her in my room. Again."

Angel stepped forward. "Just now?"

I nodded. "Yep. As soon as you left the room, I turned and there she was. How she got in, I have no idea."

"You could just ask, Jack," Wednesday noted spitefully. "You didn't have to drag me out here to the Ghost Busters."

"Shut up," I hissed then readdressed Angel. "What should we do with her?"

Jared shot me a concerned look, obviously distressed by the events unfolding before him. I ignored the snooty witch and kept my eyes on Angel.

"Call the cops I would imagine," Angel said. "Seems like the right thing to do."

That's not what I wanted to hear. I wasn't going to simply turn her in to the authorities. I glanced across the room and smiled. "No, wait. I have a better idea."

Chapter Twenty

We were ready to begin the séance.

Seated around the table, Angel was at the head and I to her right. Jazz was next to me holding my hand while Singe, Brad, and Jared were along the opposite side. All the lights in the house were off, making the only light the flickering candles in the center of the table. We could hear the storm raging outside, the wind whipping across the eaves and sleet pounding against the windows. The house was cold, and for the first time since I moved in, it was quiet...

Except for Wednesday's unhappy, albeit muffled, grunts. Shackled to the wall directly behind Angel, we had bound her feet and gagged her. It was more satisfying than I could possibly have imagined. She struggled, but wasn't going anywhere.

The looks I gathered around the table ranged from outright disgust to odd curiosity. I'm certain a few of them had begun to question my sanity. I had heard their arguments as I chained Wednesday to the wall, but couldn't care less. This was my house, my investigation, my prisoner, and my last chance. I wasn't going to let anyone—not even someone seated at this table—ruin it. I was calling the shots now.

If they wanted to leave, they were free to.

"Jack," Angel tightened her grip on my hand, "this isn't right." She leaned close to my ear and lowered her voice. "You can't hold someone against their will, no matter what they did. You are breaking the law." She paused, hoping to hear me acquiesce but when I didn't, she continued. "I don't like this, and I don't think the séance will work correctly with all this negativity in the room. Most of them hate you, and if the girl could get free, I think she would gut you on the spot. You're not very good at making friends, are you?"

"Are we going to do this or not?" I asked in a loud enough voice so that all could hear.

Angel deflated back into her seat. I felt her grip loosen for a moment as if she were deciding whether to leave or not. She looked at each face around the table in turn, then came back to mine. "Fine," she breathed.

I knew her curiosity would keep her here. She had to know, just as I had to. Angel had devoted her life to the pursuit and discovery of the paranormal. She wasn't going to let it slip through her fingers when she was this close. I was counting on that.

Jack, don't do this...

I sat straight up. My eyes careened around the table, but I couldn't tell if anyone else had heard her voice. I peered over my shoulder to catch the stink eye from Wednesday, who was still firmly gagged. I waited, holding my breath, listening. Only the sounds of fabric rustling inside and the storm outside met my ears. My heart raced. She was here. Right here. Right now. I felt emotions well up in my chest I hadn't experienced in a long, long time. This was going to work. I knew it. Not even death could keep me from her.

I squeezed Angel's hand. "Let's begin."

She nodded and smiled to reassure me.

That's when we all heard three loud knocks.

Everyone froze and the house became deathly quiet. I could practically hear each of their hearts pounding in their rib cages. The candles flickered as though a stiff wind blew through the room.

"Okay," Brad said with a quiver in his voice, "what the hell was that? Usually we don't hear noises until after the séance has started."

The group laughed nervously.

"We should start," I said to Angel excitedly.

Angel looked from me to her team then lowered her gaze, "I'm not sure. There's a lot of activity tonight." She was clearly frightened but trying to hide it. "I might not be able to control it all."

"We have to," I urged.

Three more loud knocks echoed through the house.

"I don't like this," Singe said quietly.

I shot a nasty glance at the young woman to quiet her. "What would you like?" Okay, that was a little over the top. I breathed out some of my venom and turned my attention to the ringmaster. "This is it, Angel. Start the séance!"

The room became silent again as all eyes fell on Angel. She was their fearless commander, leading the charge into battle, and if she was scared, what hope did the rest of them have? She knew that. They knew that too. She had to make a decision, and make it now.

"Hello…?"

I sat back, uncertain what I had just heard. It

180

sounded very familiar, but it couldn't be. There was simply no way—

"Jack?"

I looked up in the doorway to see Janice and my editor James standing with slack jaws.

Crap.

"Oh for fuck's sake," I said, then sighed. I dropped my head to the table with a thud that hurt more than I was prepared to admit to anyone. Fate was out to bone me tonight.

"What the hell is going on here?" James asked incredulously. "Is this one of those orgy parties I've heard about? And if so, why wasn't I invited?"

Janice had a bemused look on her face, as if she were enjoying the sight. She shifted her posture and placed her hand on her hip as a wry smile grew on her face.

I had to do damage control, and quick. Shooting up from my seat, I tried not to let anyone see me rubbing the sore spot in the middle of my forehead. Slapping my hands on James and Janice's shoulders, I then turned them, and guided the two into the foyer. "Why are you here?"

"I'm your editor," James said. "Isn't that reason enough? Can't I stop by and visit my favorite author?"

"Sorry, now is not a good time," I said, trying to push them toward the front door. "Thanks for stopping by but..." Wait, he was schmoozing, and actually being nice. Why? "What's wrong?"

"Nothing, nothing," James reassured me as he adjusted his suit jacket that I had rudely moved out of place. "Just wanted to stop by and see how the rewrites were coming."

I slowly glanced from James to Janice then back. Something was out of place. "How did you find me?"

"When I couldn't reach you by phone," Janice fielded the question, "I contacted your agent, who said you had bought a home in Union. She even gave us the address."

I was definitely getting a new agent. "Okay," I drew out the word uncomfortably, "but the question still remains why are you here?"

James adjusted his tie. "In the confusion at the end of our meeting," he cleared his throat, "I seem to have misplaced my copy of your manuscript."

I couldn't help but smile.

"I was hoping to get a new copy of it," James said. "Either hard copy or on disk, if that wouldn't be too much trouble."

I wondered if he was lying to me. Did he know I took it, or did he honestly believe he lost it? And why was he being so nice to me? I didn't think he would care if he had a copy or not after basically calling it a steaming pile of dog crap during our meeting. Something was off. Then I remembered that he had been called into the CEO's office regarding his expense account. It was time to mess with him. "Sure, I can get you a copy. Hey, you never told me, how was your trip to the Caribbean?"

James' face turned pale.

Yep. He had been bent over the CEO's desk.

"It was good," James stuttered. "How did you know about it?"

"Oh, everyone knows," I dismissed. "Say,

didn't you take that cute girl from accounting?"

James' pale complexion was starting to green.

"What was her name?" I snapped my fingers trying to remember. "Lacey? Is that right?"

James nodded. "Lacey. Her name is Lacey. Can I have the manuscript now, Jack?"

"Hold on," I said, then laughed. "Did you go scuba diving?" I leaned over and elbowed him gently in the stomach like an old college chum exchanging war stories. "Or did you two spend the whole trip at the hotel?"

"Jack," James spat my name. "I know you stole the manuscript from my office."

My smile faded.

"I was trying to be a nice guy about this." His green color was quickly being replaced by red. "I don't have time for this shit."

"I think you do," I said, studying my editor. "I think you seriously overstepped your bounds with the publisher. That's why you and Janice had to drive out to Union to see me."

James smacked his lips with an unsatisfied click. "And why is that, Mr. Ego?"

I had just been called. It was time to see if my hand beat his. "Because I think I'm the only author you have left on your docket, and if you lose me, you're out the door."

I waited while James stood silently.

It was a game of chicken.

He swerved first.

"Fine. You're right. I fucked up," he admitted. "Now you're all I've got. If I screw up with you, I'm out on the street." James stared at me angrily.

"Happy now?"

I thought for a moment and enjoyed my win, despite having to crush him to do it. I had taken all of his power, and felt good about it. "Yes actually. Thank you."

"You're an asshole," James whimpered like a bloodied kid who had just been beaten up by the school bully. "Now can I have the manuscript back?"

"Sure," I said, then chuckled and walked back into the master bedroom. I recalled the manuscript's accusing looks, and being forced to stow it in the nightstand. Moving across the room, but careful to avoid the stupid bearskin rug, I pushed my suitcase out of the way and reached for the nightstand drawer. Flashes of giant, spooky spiders gripped me, and I wondered if I would find another in the drawer. Stepping to the side, I slowly pulled out the drawer and found it completely empty. Curious... I could have sworn I put it in here. Dropping down to my knees, I lifted the bed's skirt and peered beneath. Dust bunnies roamed the open expanse, but no sign of my manuscript. I didn't think it was here, and I didn't have time to thoroughly search the room. Heading out, I started back toward the foyer.

As James and Janice's expectant gazes met mine, I shrugged. "I'll have to get you a copy tomorrow. Can't seem to find it."

James set his jaw and nodded. "Fine. Janice," he turned to his assistant, "will you make the arrangements?"

"Sure thing, Mr. Baxter," Janice said politely.

James turned and headed toward the front door.

184

He had apparently had enough fun with me for one evening.

"Jack!"

I spun on my heels to see Jazz skitter into the foyer. Clearly panicked, her eyes were wide and her chest heaving despite the short jog from the dining room. "You need to get back in there." She was visibly shaking.

I started toward her. "Why? Jazz, what's going on?" I looked past her to the wildly flickering gold light spilling out of the dining room.

Jazz shook her head and backpedaled toward the dining room. "It has Angel."

That's when I heard a scream.

Chapter Twenty-One

I stopped dead in the dining room doorway, James and Janice right behind me. Fear and déjà vu gripped me hard, unwilling to let me move or act. I had been here before.

Chairs were scattered angrily about the floor as people hadn't taken the time to push them out while trying to flee. The candelabra in the center of the table was on its side and setting fire to the tablecloth. The blaze was small, but growing quickly. Angel's team was pressed back against the walls, staring in awe. This was obviously something they had never encountered before. But I had.

Angel's body was rigid as she hovered above the table.

Her arms were spread wide and her back arched angrily with her face tilted toward the roof as though she were about to be crucified on the cross. Blue sparkles of electricity popped and crackled around her body as her clothes and hair fluttered. Objects spun around her like a mini solar system, gradually picking up speed as they orbited. Her hands convulsed and shook as her fingers bent at wild, unnatural angles. Angel's head snapped forward, her face a mixture of pain and fear, then back with an audible crunch. She was moaning, though it sounded as if two separate voices were competing for control. The entity was trying to possess her, and she was again trying to fight it, though it looked like she was losing.

Damn.

"What the fuck is happening?" I heard James ask from behind me, but his question sounded distant like he was miles away.

Rushing toward the flames, something in me snapped. I acted before my brain could figure out what I was doing and attempt to stop me. Scooping up one of Angel's new plants, I dumped the potting soil on the fire to try and douse it. "Jared!"

The witch snapped his head toward me. His face was a portrait of pure terror. That wasn't a good sign.

"Throw some Harry Potter shit at Angel," I yelled over the moaning and roar of the fire.

I wasn't sure it was possible, but his eyes opened wider in confusion. "What?"

Tossing the empty planter away, I grabbed another plant and threw it on the fire. I think I was only succeeding in feeding the flames. I turned my attention back to Jared. "You're a witch! Do something! Help Angel!"

As if he had been slapped, he gained composure from the words. Jared nodded once. "Right." Snapping his robe down with confidence, he snatched his chunk of sage from Angel's orbit and lit it with the flames on the table. Springing onto the table, the witch stood fast before Angel and began to chant.

"Jazz, Brad!" I yelled, throwing the pot to the floor.

The two turned to look at me.

"Fire extinguisher," I instructed, watching the flames steadily grow out of control before me. "Or water. Get something!"

Filled with a confidence from Jared's actions, the two shot off the wall and darted for the kitchen.

"Singe," I looked up to see the young woman cowering in the corner. She wasn't staring at Angel, but the quickly spreading flames. It took a moment to register, but it finally hit me. Her burns… "Shit."

I reached behind and grabbed James. "See that girl?" I asked, pointing to Singe. "Help her. Now!"

"What the hell do you want me to do?" His pupils were black with terror. "I'm not going in that fucking room!"

"I'll go," Janice said without hesitation. Moving around me, she pulled her arm up to guard her face from the flames and flying debris.

"Good girl." I smiled as Janice reached Singe and helped her out of the corner. Pushing my useless editor away, I turned my attention to—

Double damn.

Wednesday was gone. The shackles hung empty on the wall. But I couldn't deal with that now.

Lightning flashed outside and the ensuing thunder shook the walls of the house.

Turning back to Jared, I spun around the table just as Brad charged back in with a small red fire extinguisher. Vaulting off a fallen chair I leapt onto the table next to the witch just as Jazz entered with another extinguisher. As Brad and Jazz attacked the flames, I grabbed Jared's hand and listened to his words. I could feel the heat of the flames scorching the hairs on my arms. Focusing all of my attention, I quickly memorized his chant and joined in.

Angel's head snapped forward again, her face

contorted with what I could only guess was pure rage. Her lips peeled back over her gritted teeth showing a horrid milky red smear of blood on the enamel. Her sclerae and pupils were completely gone, absorbed by an inky blackness that seemed hollow and reflected no light.

It wasn't Angel.

"Who are you?" I shouted.

One of her beefy paws swatted at my head, but quickly snapped back. Angel was still in there, still fighting. This was borrowed time.

Ducking down, Jared barely avoided a careening book meant for his skull. He continued to chant, louder and louder. Using the smoking sage, he made a continuous pentacle sign in front of Angel.

I stared down the entity. "I demand to know who you are!"

It growled at me, but refused to answer. Gnashing its teeth, the entity reared back and spit.

Angel's blood smacked against my face. Trying to wipe it away, I think I only succeeded in smearing it across my cheek. I stood fast.

The entity cocked its head slightly and regarded Jared unblinking. Its lips contorted into a horrible smile, as a streak of blood ran down from the corner of its mouth. "You fear me," it said in a guttural voice that seemed impossible for a human to create. It was as if a choir of demons spoke all at once creating a devilish cacophony, and underneath it all I could still hear Angel screaming.

"We do not fear you," I argued, though I was lying. I was scared shitless right now. "Who are you?"

"I am many!" the entity roared. "I am the alpha and the omega."

It was goading me, and it was working. My temper flared. "I don't have time for this cryptic bullshit! Tell me who you are then leave this woman! Tell me!"

In my anger, I didn't see the entity's hand move. Angel's hand swung out and caught me on the right cheek with her nails. I felt a surge of pain in my face and I stumbled back. Twisting away from the flames, I fell to the floor with a thump and clamped my hand to my cheek. My ribs screamed in pain as I further aggravated them.

Gritting my teeth, I lifted off the floor. I could not, no, I would not stay down. Pulling my hand away from my cheek, I stared angrily at a dark smear of blood across my fingers and palm. After taking a breath to calm myself, I stepped back onto the table and faced the entity again. My body ached. I was bruised and broken, but I would not stay down.

"Who are you?" I yelled.

The entity stared at me, blood running down from its maniacally grinning lips. It regarded me for a moment then redirected its attention past me. Fear settled in my stomach like a writhing ball of snakes, each taking turns biting the lining of my stomach as they tried to free themselves. I heard someone behind me choking.

Turning slowly, I found Wednesday holding James in a submission hold, a glittering silver blade pressed to his throat. The only thing that popped into my mind was she could have picked a better hostage.

"Wednesday," I breathed her name, "let James go and put down the knife. You don't have to do this." My mind swam with possibilities. Was she a conduit like Angel? Had the entity possessed her?

"You never listen to me, Jack!" Wednesday shouted and twisted James' arm behind his back. "I was here to help you."

"Get this crazy bitch off me!" James croaked.

Wednesday held the blade so hard to James' throat that I saw blood well up around it. "I'm listening now," I assured her as I stepped off the table. "Help me."

I could hear the entity laughing.

"It's too late, Jack." I watched a bloody tear roll down her cheek.

"No," I said. I walked past Brad and Jazz as they finally extinguished the last of the flames. They stepped behind me, watching my back. "Please, don't do this."

"I don't have a choice," she whispered. "I can't fight it anymore."

I shuddered. The entity did have her. "You wanted to help me," I chose my words carefully, "now it's my turn. Let me help you, Wednesday." I stopped short of her and held out my hands in a gesture of respect. "Give me the knife." I looked her straight in the eyes. "Please. Let me help you."

A horrible sneer appeared on Wednesday's face.

With one quick motion, she pulled the blade free and stepped back. James grabbed his neck as blood spurted free, gagged, and fell writhing to the floor. As blood pooled around his head, he shuddered one final time then stopped. James was dead.

"Jack." Wednesday laughed as she cleaned James' blood off her blade on the shoulder of her black shirt. "You're a moron."

I stared in dread at the evil marionette. "What the fuck is wrong with you?"

"You just don't get it. I thought you would figure it out, but I overestimated you. I gave you too much credit," Wednesday rambled.

I wanted to charge her, to wring her tiny neck. I wanted to feel her windpipe collapse beneath my hands as I choked her to death. I gritted my teeth.

She pointed over my shoulder, curling her hand into the shape of a gun. Cocking her thumb down, she pulled the imaginary trigger.

I heard a scream then a crash.

Spinning, I watched everyone rushing toward where Angel had fallen. It was a diversion. The entity hadn't possessed Angel. It was—

Oh fuck.

I felt the blade of Wednesday's knife pierce my back just to the right of my spine. Gasping in pain, she twisted it. I heard the blade scrape bone as she pushed it in harder. Sliding her arm slowly around my neck, the evil marionette slithered up to my back. Her grip was like steel. As my throat started to collapse under the pressure, I saw black spots before my eyes.

"Jack." I could feel her cold lips against my ear. "I was going to help you, but instead I'm going to kill you. That's just the way these things go." Her tongue flicked out and ran up my earlobe. "Sorry, Sweetheart."

Chapter Twenty-Two

Rage roared unchecked through my body while endorphins temporarily masked the pain of the knife. I had all I could take of this place. Balling my fists, I summoned every bit of strength I had. This was going to hurt. A lot.

I snapped my head back and felt it connect with the bridge of her nose. She screamed as blood splattered on the back of my neck but I felt her grip loosen. Twisting against Wednesday and quickly drawing a breath, I spun and connected with her chin first with my elbow then the back of my fist. The blade ripped free of my back and the evil marionette slammed into the wall.

My lower back shrieked in agony, and I think I was yelling but couldn't be sure. A fog of pain and anger had settled on my brain. It felt like a huge canyon was open in my flesh and my organs would simply slip out and plop on the floor. I could feel the warmth of my blood running down the back of my leg. Using my fingers to apply pressure, I hoped I could stem the bleeding. Feeling the jagged edges of the wound, I felt my stomach gurgle and flop in disgust.

"Fuck, Jack," Wednesday said as she wiped the blood away from her nose with the back of her hand, "that really hurt."

I pulled my bloody hand free of my back and showed it to her. "And this didn't? You stabbed me!"

Wednesday shrugged.

194

"We need the paramedics!" I heard Brad's voice shout.

I quickly glanced over my shoulder to see Angel's team lifting her off the floor. Her face was bloody and her eyes were rolled back in her head. She looked like she was dead.

Turning back, I swallowed hard. Crap.

Wednesday was gone.

Again.

Jack, the window!

That time I was sure it was Irene's voice. I stood quietly waiting, secretly thinking that if I sat down, I would never get back up again, but there were no more warnings to follow.

My eyes fell on James' dead body at my feet. A pool of blood had collected around his head where Wednesday had cut him from ear to ear. His face was still contorted into a look of sheer terror, and would be until rigor mortis set in. I didn't like the guy, but I hadn't wished this on him. He was a good man, but somehow he had gotten too big for his britches. Power had a way of doing that. Absolutely. Kneeling down before my editor, my back screamed in protest. Pain skittered up my spine like electricity and exploded into my brain. Sucking in a deep breath, I fought it with everything I had left.

Reaching down, I pushed James' eyelids closed. "Bye, buddy."

Slowly standing, I turned back to Angel and her team. They had carefully placed the large woman on the table and were trying to make her comfortable. Jared was sitting on the table next to her, his hand on her chest and chanting slowly. Behind them, I saw Janice and Singe walk back into the room, a blanket draped over Singe's shoulders.

Jazz placed her fingers on Angel's forehead and closed her eyes. "She's still in there," Jazz confirmed. The conduit looked up to me with a deep sadness on her face. "I can hear her screaming."

Lightning flashed as the storm raged ominously outside.

I dug my cell phone out of my pocket and tossed it to Brad. "Call an ambulance."

Brad nodded and started to dial.

Janice rushed around the table and stood at my side. "Oh my god, Mr. Devlin," she said, noting the ever-growing red bloodstain on my shirt. "Are you okay?"

I grunted to confirm, although I wasn't exactly sure.

Janice dropped to her knees. "Mr. Baxter." She reached out to touch James, but couldn't bring herself to actually make contact. She pulled back her shaking hand and cradled it. Spotting the knife where Wednesday dropped it, she turned and shot me a hateful, accusing look.

Lifting my hand, I took a step back. "I didn't do this, Janice. You know me. I didn't kill James."

Her glare didn't soften. Slowly standing, she moved away from me, carefully keeping her back to the wall.

"Janice," I whispered. "How can you even think I did this?"

"Stay away from me," Janice hissed. "I want out of this place."

I started to argue—

196

"Now!" Janice roared.

Feeling too weak to argue or stop her, I took a pain-filled breath and stepped out of Janice's way. She rushed past me without another word, heading straight for the front door.

Brad snapped my cell phone shut and held it out to me. "Paramedics and police are on their way."

Accepting the phone, I nodded. "You guys stay here with Angel."

Jazz took a step toward me with a worried expression. She already knew, I think even before I did, what I was going to do. "You can't stop this. Not alone."

"The hell I can't." I put on my best smile. "I've already made up my mind. Don't try to argue with me."

Jazz nodded and stepped back. She hung her head and returned to Angel's side.

Well, they could have argued with me a little bit at least. Somebody could have said, No, Jack, don't go! Don't do it! But did they? Nope.

Nice.

Turning away from the team of paranormal investigators, I snatched Wednesday's knife off the floor, and hobbled into the octagonal family room. Every step felt like a nuclear explosion of pain in my back. As each foot fell, my body urged me to lie down on the floor and close my eyes. I just wanted to rest. But I couldn't. I finally understood what was going on in the house, and there was work to be done. I slipped the knife into my back pocket.

Not to be too melodramatic or anything, but I

had to stop it.

Chapter Twenty-Three

Limping through the octagonal family room, I felt eyes burning into my back much the same way as the first time I entered The Hollow. My problems had started the moment I stepped foot in this godforsaken place, and they weren't going to stop until I was dead. Despite being certain that moment was fast approaching as my vision dimmed, I wasn't going out without a fight. Although I had been seeking the dead for the past two years, I wasn't anxious to join their ranks just yet.

Stepping into the foyer, I shivered. It was like an icebox, despite being as warm as the rest of the house only minutes before. Exhaling, I saw my breath freeze in the air. The massive windows on the stairs were illuminating the room with an eerie blue haze that couldn't have been natural. Rain washed down the windows creating odd shadows that blobbed and crawled over the room like germs. Lightning flashed blinding me for a moment, but I was certain I saw the shape of a figure on the stairs. And it wasn't Wednesday. The foyer retook its blue hue as the lightning vanished and thunder rumbled from the clouds, showing me that I was still alone.

Walking toward the stairs, I felt a vicious pinch in my spine and my legs gave out beneath me. I tumbled and hit my head with a hard smack on the wood floor. Stars sparkled before my eyes as my entire body cried in agony. I shivered again, but the cold floor felt good against my face. I didn't want to get up. I wondered if it would just be easier to lay here and die... My body wanted to give up. Why wouldn't I let it? It all seemed so easy. I could just close my eyes and the pain would go away. I wanted the pain to go away.

Gritting my teeth, I pulled my hands under me and pushed off the floor.

Lightning flashed again.

My eyes locked on the figure before me, but I was too tired and abused to jump away. He regarded me with angry, hollow eyes, but I wasn't the reason he was there. Looking past me, the figure's strong features melted into a sneer dripping with venom. Bringing his hatchet up, the figure turned and walked straight through me.

I rolled on my back to see the foyer lit with the yellow shimmer of gas lamps. It looked slightly different than I remembered as the architecture had changed. Through the door to the family room I could no longer see octagonal walls, nor an exit to the dining room. The only remaining features were the stairs and massive glass windows behind them. This is how The Hollow once looked, back when Lincoln Ezekiel was its sole occupant and everything was new. I was witnessing the past.

Several Indian braves stood at the base of the steps, their hands dipped in blood. The figure who had walked through me stopped behind them, spoke in their native language then turned away. As each of the braves followed, I saw their faces were drawn and their heads hung low. There was no honor in what had been done, and each man knew it. And as each was dressed similarly, I got the distinct feeling this wasn't an action sanctioned by the tribe elders.

They had stopped the white man from claiming anymore of their sacred places, but it had come at a cost. They had hopefully ensured that future generations could be blessed and interred there, but not themselves. It was almost heartbreaking.

As the last brave walked away, I saw the source of their displeasure. Lincoln Ezekiel, stripped completely naked, hands and feet lashed to the banisters, was dead on the stairs. His chest was ripped open, exposing the bones of his ribs and his internal organs. A gaping hole in the upper right side was where his heart used to be. His mustached face was twisted into almost the same horrible expression I had seen on James' earlier. Ezekiel had been alive when his heart was removed.

A circle of blood had been created around him, holding in the magic they worked. This was a ritual older than any of them that was more akin to their Aztec brethren than the Iroquois. Yet they had dug up old magic to protect themselves and future generations of Cayugan. They had done what they felt was completely necessary. These were a proud people, and had been forced to extraordinary measures. They had forsaken The Hollow for generations to come. No soul that ever called this place home would find peace. They had made certain of it.

Exhaustion hit me like a tsunami. I tried not to crumble to the floor as everything around me succumbed to darkness. I was about to die. My eyes focused on the stairs. I recognized a person sitting there, lanky, swathed in black, and watching me. It was Wednesday.

Darkness claimed me.

Chapter Twenty-Four

"…Wake up, Jack."

I wanted to open my eyes, but couldn't seem to get them to cooperate. I hurt. A lot. It seemed as though every inch of my body was radiating pain to my brain. I didn't want to move or breathe as it hurt too much. Why couldn't I just die?

"Because I'm not done with you, Jack." I heard loud footsteps rush across the floor toward me then my cheek sizzled as I took a hard slap across the face. "Now open your fucking eyes!"

Wednesday…

Finally able to open them, I stared into her huge eyes as she squatted over me. There was still blood covering her mouth and chin from my reverse headbutt, but her eyes were calm and collected. She regarded me like a child staring at a bug who was about to have its legs torn off.

I didn't know where I was, but I had the distinct feeling I was still in The Hollow. "What are you?" It was the first, and only, question that came to me.

Wednesday sat on my stomach causing pain to arc through me. "I am what your religion would call a Golem," she answered coolly. "I am the unreal made real."

I understood. "You aren't a real person. You are a physical manifestation of the Cayugan curse." I licked my cracked, dry lips. "You are The Hollow."

"Ding, ding!" Wednesday said with zeal. "You just answered the fifty thousand dollar question,

Jack! Care to try the lightning round?"

I stared at the evil Marionette. She was flesh and blood, but not a denizen of this reality. She wasn't tied to the physics of our realm, which explained how she could appear and disappear at will. Somehow the Cayugan had given The Hollow sentience, and the desire to kill, but it had evolved into something more. "But how?"

"The how is boring," Wednesday said. "It took years, cobbling together bits of flesh, sawdust and nails, but I finally became reality. Do you know what it's like being a house? This form," she caressed her arms, "is so much more fun! And now I have you to play with. It's been almost twelve years since I had someone in The Hollow. I was starting to go a bit crazy."

Starting to go crazy? I think The Hollow had dove off the deep end a long, long time ago. I guess when your sole purpose in life is to kill people, you tend to go a little batty. Something didn't make sense though. "Why were you offering to help me?"

Wednesday stood off me, clasped her hands behind her back, and started to pace around me. "I was trying something new with you, Jack. Usually someone moves in, I kill them, then I have to wait for the whole process to start over. This time," she smiled, "I wanted to prolong it. I thought maybe we could team up, start a boarding house, and kill everyone who came to stay. But no! You didn't want to play, so I had to smack your bitch ass around."

"You were lonely," I said, ignoring her last comment about me being a bitch.

Wednesday didn't reply.

It was amazing. This place, created to kill all of its occupants, became so efficient at it that it was actually lonely between tenants. It was absolutely astounding. I thought for a moment...that would make a good book, should I survive this.

"So whaddya say, Jack?" Wednesday dropped down next to me Indian style. "Want to be my buddy?"

I laughed out loud, despite how much it hurt, and slid my hand down my back. "You are out of your fucking mind, Wednesday."

The evil golem hopped on my chest and pressed her hands to my shoulders. "That wasn't the answer I wanted. I guess I'm going to have to kill you and start over. I've learned one thing in two hundred years, Jack," she leaned close to my face, "how to be patient."

I would not let this place hurt anyone else.

I threw my head forward and cracked her nose again. As she reeled back with a yelp, I bucked her off, drew the knife out of my back pocket, and threw myself on her. Without a moment's hesitation, I brought the blade down with a flash. I stabbed her, the knife making the same sound it would cutting into a cantaloupe. All the rage, all the anger, and all the pain she had caused me poured out of my body. I pulled the knife free and plunged it into her flesh again and again.

Rolling back, I stared at the red mess on the floor that was Wednesday. I had ruptured both of her eyes, stabbed her in the direct center of her forehead, and her chest was a bloody puddle from the numerous wounds. Still holding the knife in my hand, I scooted away as her blood pooled around her.

She wasn't moving.

But that didn't mean anything.

I quickly glanced about trying to get my bearings amidst the immense pain in my back. My stomach was a mess of knots and bile threatening to reverse on me at any moment. The room was dark except for a small, circular window at each end that I recognized. Arching up on both sides, the ceiling matched the roof of the house. I was in the attic, but why here? Why did she drag me all the way up three flights of stairs?

Grabbing onto the wall, I carefully lifted myself up. Pain surged up and down my back, into my legs, and finally erupted into my brain. I lurched forward and threw up everything inside of me. As the first wave stopped, I coughed until I vomited again. With every cough, every contraction of my stomach muscles, my back throbbed with pain. My eyes bleary, I tried to take a breath and hold myself against the wall. Letting my head fall back, I prayed—to whoever, or whatever would listen—for strength.

I spotted the attic door on the far side. It was only a few feet from me, but it seemed like miles.

Using the wall for support, I limped painfully, and slowly, around the edge of the attic carefully ducking my head under low rafters. If I cut across, it would be quicker, though I risked falling. This path was slower, but safer. At least I had something firm to hold. Finally reaching the door, I stowed the knife in my back pocket again and grabbed the door handle. Twisting it, I heard the mechanism click free. I sighed with relief and pulled...

But the door wouldn't budge.

I yanked hard and felt pain rage like fire up my back. I wasn't about to do that again. I twisted the handle again and clearly heard it click, still the door refused to open. Scanning the door, I found no signs of it being nailed shut, or anything visible binding it. I leaned over and stared at the space between the door and frame and found what was at least an eighth of an inch gap. There should be nothing holding the door closed.

Then it occurred to me. There wasn't a way out...for any of us.

Behind me I heard scraping.

I slowly turned, already knowing what I would see.

Wednesday slithered painfully toward me, blood spilling out of her as she moved. She lumbered slowly and unsteadily. Her arms dragged at her sides as though they were useless. The two gaping holes I had created in her eye sockets oozed a thick, yellowish fluid down her cheeks. "Jack, that wasn't very nice," the evil marionette warbled through the blood that fell from her lips.

"I can't get away," I asked her, "can I?"

She tried to laugh, but instead regurgitated blood. She shook her head and continued toward me.

Jack...

I heard Irene's voice again. I remained calm. "I'm not only trying to escape you, but The

Hollow," I said.

"We are one," Wednesday gurgled.

"And if I kill you," I theorized, "I still have to deal with the house. There's no way out, is there?"

Wednesday stopped before me and wavered as though she were about to fall over. "No, Jack. There is no escape. Unless you want to reconsider our offer?"

Jack…the window.

I turned and looked at the small circular window at the end of the attic, unsure what Irene was trying to tell me. I had to buy a little more time. "What if you die?"

"I will be recreated," Wednesday said. She stared at me through bloody eye sockets. "It has happened before, it will happen again."

…The Window.

I looked again at the window, but still didn't understand.

"I'm just so lonely, Jack," Wednesday breathed. "I need you."

Her statement clicked inside of my weary, pain-filled brain. I knew in that moment what Irene had been trying to tell me, and what the solution was. It all made sense. "Thank you, Irene."

Taking a deep breath, I turned and ran. Pain surged through my body, and it felt as though my feet were cinder blocks, but I ran. The evil marionette lunged for my legs, but missed and hit the floor. With every movement, my body screamed in agony. I was dying.

I heard Wednesday scream in defeat.

Bringing my arms up across my head, I leaned

208

forward and tossed myself at the small window. The glass and wood scraped and bit into my flesh as I broke through, as though The Hollow knew this was its last chance to hold onto me. Free of the window, I felt myself weightless in the midst of the storm for a moment. I saw the heavy clouds above ripple with lightning, and the approaching red and blue lights of emergency vehicles below. Rain pelted into my flesh and wind whipped around me.

I was free.

It was over.

In that moment, I knew Irene hadn't left me. She had been by my side all along, protecting me.

My body arced down toward the wet ground.

And I fell.

Chapter Twenty-Five

"...And as you can see, we've had to heavily sedate him."

I heard a woman's voice choke back a sob, obviously distressed at the news. But who was talking?

"He was a danger to himself and the staff."

My mind was drowning in confusion. I remembered falling and hurtling toward the rain-soaked ground, but I couldn't recall the impact. I felt nauseous, as though I wanted to vomit, but, somehow, I didn't hurt. The pain in my back and ribs was completely gone. I tried to roll onto my side but couldn't. Opening my eyes, my optic nerves tried to process the white blur before them. I could vaguely make out shapes, but there were no defining details. My mouth was dry as if packed with cotton. I smacked my lips to create saliva, but the sick feeling in my gut only worsened. I felt totally helpless. Had I survived my escape from The Hollow, but somehow been terribly injured? That was the only thing that made sense. I was still alive. That was, at least, something.

Where was I?

"Is he ever going to be himself again, Doctor?"

That voice...but how was it possible? I knew it, every nuance of it, yet it seemed so alien and out of context. It couldn't be.

I snapped my head toward the sound of her voice and tried to force my eyes to focus, but felt as though they were covered with gauze.

"I don't know, Ms. Devlin," the doctor replied.

I heard the woman openly sob. "Oh my God. Jack."

"Irene?" I said.

I felt soft, feminine fingers slip around my hand. "I'm here, sweetheart."

This didn't feel right. "How are you, I mean, aren't you…" I wanted to ask, but the words died in my throat. She was dead. I knew it. I held her in my arms as she died, yet I could hear her voice, and feel her fingers holding my hand. It was like I was trapped in some horrible, horrible dream. "Where am I?"

Silence.

"Irene?" My vision still wouldn't clear. I posed the question again. "Where am I?"

I felt her grip tighten. "Archview."

The name snapped in my mind like a rubber band. Instantly it conjured up deep, dark images I wasn't prepared to deal with. The name was more chilling to me than any spook or specter could ever be. This wasn't just a dream, it was a full-blown nightmare.

"Archview," I repeated, making sure I had heard her correctly. "Archview Asylum?"

Silence again.

"Irene," I said more forcefully, "tell me!"

"Yes," she said, a definite quiver in her voice.

This time it was my turn to be speechless.

"You've been committed," she said finally. "You just kept ranting about some girl named Wednesday, The Hollow, and ghosts," Irene added almost crying. "Then you claimed I was dead."

"That really happened!" I tried to sit up again, but realized I was in ankle and wrist restraints. "You committed suicide! I moved to Union, New York to find a haunted house. I wanted to make contact with you."

"No, Jack." Irene struggled. "You're in Idaho. We're in Boise, not New York."

"Yes," I said, remembering where Archview was. "We are now. But I was in New York! In a house called The Hollow."

"No, Jack," Irene said again.

"I met a paranormal investigator named Angel Arroyo and her team. Janice and James were there." Oh God…James was dead. It hit me like a semi-truck at full speed as if I had somehow forgotten it. I had watched him die by Wednesday's hand. Maybe that was it! They thought I had something to do with his death…? "Wednesday killed James. There were witnesses—"

"James isn't dead," Irene cut me off. "I spoke with him on the phone this morning."

The confusion in my brain only deepened. How was he alive? How was Irene alive, for that matter? What the hell was going on here? Had I somehow jumped out of The Hollow and into the Twilight Zone?

"I don't understand," I finally admitted. "All my memories…they all seem so real."

"It's because they are," Irene offered, "in a way. You created them."

I closed my eyes and stopped trying to fight the blur. I was completely and utterly lost. "What are you talking about?"

212

"Your book," Irene whispered, "Jessie's Warning."

I thought about my most recent novel, but still didn't make the connection.

"This happened in the book," my wife explained. "The main character is a writer whose wife commits suicide. He tries to contact her via Electronic Voice Phenomenon in haunted houses. His search leads him to Union, New York…"

"Where he finds a house called The Hollow, and a mysterious gothic girl he dubs Wednesday," I finished.

It was true. I remembered it all so clearly now. To escape The Hollow, the main character jumps out the window to his death, just as I remembered myself doing. All of my memories…all of my experiences…everything that had happened was fabricated by my mind.

No.

I would not accept that. It had happened. I was there. This was all a fantasy, not what happened in Union. I had not imagined the whole thing. It was all too vivid in my brain. I could remember the sounds, the smells, and the taste of the memories. This wasn't right.

"Irene." I tried to lift my hand again to no avail. Angered, I struggled against the wrist restraints. "Irene, you have to get me out of here! This isn't right. That really happened! I was at The Hollow!"

I heard my wife cry again, "Stop it, Jack! Stop it!"

"Help me, Irene! Like you did in the house!" I tried to kick free of my ankle straps. "You told me to jump out the window to stop Wednesday, and I did! You saved me!"

"Stop, Jack!" Irene screamed at the top of her lungs. "It wasn't real! None of it!"

"Help me," I cried. I must have looked like a fish out of water flopping and writhing on the bed.

"Sedate this man," I heard the doctor order.

I felt hands on my chest and legs then the full body weight of several nurses and orderlies. I struggled wildly against them, but they succeeded in holding me down. Gritting my teeth, I felt a sharp sting in my shoulder then the warm sensation of the sedative spreading through my tissues. It was only seconds before my body became weak and numb. I started to fade. I tried to hold on for just a moment longer.

"He's going to be out for a while," I heard the doctor say. "You can come back later if you like."

"Thank you," Irene answered. I heard her footsteps start to walk away, but she stopped. "Oh, and, Doctor?"

"Yes, Ms. Devlin?"

"When Jack wakes up," Irene's voice was quiet and collected, "could you tell him that Jessie's Warning just made the best seller's list?"

I closed my eyes and let the darkness take me.

www.ingramcontent.com/pod-product-compliance
Lightning Source LLC
Chambersburg PA
CBHW011500170626
46814CB00008B/2985

* 9 7 8 1 7 8 6 9 5 6 9 1 0 *